This couldn't be happening.

She couldn't really be kissing the chief of police.

No, it was real enough. She seemed hyperaware of each of her senses. He tasted of cocoa and hot male and he smelled like laundry soap and starch and a very sexy aftershave with wood and musk notes. As she had expected, Trace Bowman kissed like a man who knew exactly how to cherish a woman, who would make sure she always felt safe and cared for in his arms. He explored her mouth as if he wanted to taste every millimeter of it and wouldn't rest until he knew every single one of her secrets.

Dear Reader,

I don't know about you, but Christmas at my house is all about easy. With a packed calendar of parties, shopping, wrapping and generalized chaos, I try to find the simplest ways to do things while still enjoying some favorite traditions. This recipe is perfect for those of you who (like me!) love homemade candy but not all the fuss. All my best to you and yours this joyous season.

EASY VANILLA MICROWAVE CARAMELS

4 tbsp butter
1 cup brown sugar
½ cup corn syrup
2/3 cup sweetened condensed milk
1 tsp vanilla
butter (for greasing pan)
nonstick aluminum foil or parchment paper
waxed paper, cut into 4"–5" squares

Butter an 8" x 8" pan. Line the pan with nonstick foil or parchment paper, folding any excess over the outside edges; set aside. Mix the butter, brown sugar and corn syrup in a microwave-safe glass bowl or measuring cup. Microwave on High for two minutes. Stir mixture and return to microwave for two minutes. Add sweetened condensed milk and stir well. Microwave for 3½ minutes. Remove from microwave and stir in vanilla. Pour into prepared pan, scraping any residue from the sides of the bowl. Set aside and let cool to room temperature. When the caramel has cooled, remove liner from the pan. Cut into approximately 1" squares with a well-buttered knife. Butter your hands well, then place one caramel in the middle of a waxed-paper square. Roll the paper into a cylinder and twist the ends. Store the wrapped candies in a cool, dry place.

RaeAnne

CHRISTMAS IN COLD CREEK

RAEANNE THAYNE

Harlequin®

SPECIAL EDITION

PLEASE RECYCLE · THIS PRODUCT IS RECYCLABLE

Recycling programs
for this product may
not exist in your area.

ISBN-13: 978-0-373-65631-8

CHRISTMAS IN COLD CREEK

Copyright © 2011 by RaeAnne Thayne

This edition published by arrangement with Harlequin Books S.A.

For questions and comments about the quality of this book please contact us at Customer_eCare@Harlequin.ca.

® and TM are trademarks of Harlequin Books S.A., used under license. Trademarks indicated with ® are registered in the United States Patent and Trademark Office, the Canadian Trade Marks Office and in other countries.

www.Harlequin.com

Printed in U.S.A.

Recent books by RaeAnne Thayne

RAEANNE THAYNE

finds inspiration in the beautiful northern Utah mountains, where she lives with her husband and three children. Her books have won numerous honors, including RITA® Award nominations from Romance Writers of America and a Career Achievement Award from *RT Book Reviews*. RaeAnne loves to hear from readers and can be contacted through her website, www.raeannethayne.com.

To Sarah Stone, our angel, for a year full of adventure. We can't thank you enough!

Chapter One

Much as he loved Pine Gulch, Trace Bowman had to admit his town didn't offer its best impression in the middle of a cold, gray rain that leached the color and personality from it.

Even the Christmas decorations—which still somehow could seem magical and bright to his cynical eye when viewed on a snowy December evening—somehow came off looking only old and tired in the bleak late-November morning light as he parked his patrol SUV in front of The Gulch, the diner that served as the town's central gathering place.

That sleety rain dripping from the eaves and awnings of the storefronts would be snow by late afternoon, he guessed. Maybe earlier. This time of year—the week after Thanksgiving—in Pine Gulch, Idaho, in the western shadow of the Tetons, snow was more the norm than the exception.

He yawned and rotated his neck to ease some of the tightness and fatigue. After three days of double shifts, he was ready to head for his place a few blocks away, throw a big, thick log on the fire and climb into bed for the next week or so.

Food first. He'd eaten a quick sandwich for dinner around 6:00 p.m. More than twelve hours—and the misery of dealing with a couple of weather-related accidents—later and he was craving one of Lou Archuleta's sumptuous cinnamon rolls. Sleep could wait a half hour for him to fill up his tank.

He walked in and was hit by a welcome warmth and the smell of frying bacon and old coffee. From the tin-stamped ceiling to the row of round swivel seats at the old-fashioned counter, The Gulch fit every stereotype of the perfect small-town diner. The place oozed tradition and constancy. He figured if he moved away for twenty years, The Gulch would seem the same the moment he walked back through the doors.

"Morning, Chief!" Jesse Redbear called out from the booth reserved for the diner's regulars.

"Hey, Jesse."

"Chief."

"Chief."

Greetings assailed him from the rest of the booth, from Mick Malone and Sal Martinez and Patsy Halliday. He could probably have squeezed into their corner booth but he still headed for an empty stool at the counter.

He waved at them all and continued his quick scan of the place, an old habit from his days as a military MP that still served him well. He recognized everyone in the room except for a couple he thought might be staying at the hotel and a girl reading a book in the corner. She looked to be his niece, Destry's, age and he had to wonder what a nine-year-old girl was doing by herself at The Gulch at 7:30 a.m. on a school day.

Then he noticed a slender woman standing at one of the back booths with an order pad in her hand. Since when did The Gulch have a new waitress? He'd been busy working double shifts after the wife of one of his men had a baby and he hadn't been in for a week or two, but last he knew, Donna Archuleta, the wife of the owner, seemed to handle the breakfast crowd fine on her own. Maybe she was finally slowing down now that she'd hit seventy.

"Hey, Chief," Lou Archuleta, Donna's husband and the cook, called out from behind the grill before Trace could ask Donna about the solitary girl or the new waitress. "Long night?"

How did Lou know he'd been working all night? Was he wearing a sign or something? Maybe the man just figured it out from his muddy boots and the exhaustion he was pretty sure was probably stamped on his features.

"It was a rough one. That freezing rain always keeps us hopping. I've been helping the state police out on the highway with a couple of weather-related accidents."

"You ought to be home in bed catching up." Donna, skinny and feisty, flipped a cup over and poured coffee into it for him. The last thing he needed was caffeine when he wanted to be asleep in about five minutes from now, but he decided not to make an issue of it.

"That's my plan, but I figured I'd sleep better on a full stomach."

"You want your regular?" she asked in her raspy ex-smoker's voice. "Western omelet and a stack?"

He shook his head. "No stack. I'm in the mood for one of Lou's sweet rolls this morning. Any left?"

"I think I can find one or two for our favorite man in blue."

"Thanks."

He eased his tired bones onto a stool and caught a better look at the new waitress. She was pretty and slender with dark hair pulled back in a haphazard sort of ponytail. More curious than he probably should be, he noted her white blouse seemed to be tailored and expensive. The hand holding a coffeepot was soft-looking with manicured nails.

What was someone in designer jeans doing serving coffee at The Gulch?

And not well, he noted as she splattered Maxwell House over the lip of Ronny Haskell's coffee cup. Ronny didn't seem to mind. He just smiled, somewhere in the vicinity of her chest region.

"Do you want something else to drink?" Donna asked him, apparently noticing he hadn't lifted his cup.

He gave her a rueful smile. "To be honest, I need sleep more than caffeine today. A small orange juice will do me."

"I should have thought about that. One OJ coming up."

She headed toward the small grill window to give his order to her husband and returned a minute later with his juice. Her hand shook a little as she set it down and he noted more signs of how Donna and Lou were both growing older. Maybe that's why they'd added a server to help with the breakfast crowd.

"Busy morning," he commented to Donna when she came back with the sweet roll, huge and gooey and warm.

"Let me tell you something. I've survived my share of Pine Gulch winters," she said. "In my experience, gloomy days like this make people either want to hunker down at home by themselves in front of the fire or seek out other people. Guess we've got more of the latter today."

The new waitress eased up to the window and tentatively handed an order to Lou before heading back to take the order of a couple of new arrivals.

"Who's the new blood?" he asked with a little head jerk in her direction.

Donna stopped just short of rolling her eyes. "Name's Parsons. Rebecca Parsons. But heaven forbid you make the mistake of calling her Becky. It's *Becca.* Apparently she inherited old Wally Taylor's place. His granddaughter, I guess."

That was news to Trace. He narrowed his gaze at the woman, suddenly put off. Wally had never spoken of a granddaughter. She sure hadn't been overflowing with concern for the old man. In his last few years, Trace had just about been his neighbor's only visitor. If he hadn't made a practice of checking on him a couple of times a week, Wally might have gone weeks without seeing another living soul.

Trace had been the first to find out that he'd passed away. When Trace hadn't seen him puttering around his yard for a couple of days or out with his grumpy mutt, Grunt, he'd stopped by to check and found him dead in his easy chair with the Game Show Network still on, Grunt whining at his feet.

Apparently his granddaughter had been too busy to come visit him but she hadn't blinked at moving in and taking over his house. It would serve her right if he dropped Grunt off for her. Lord knew he didn't need a grouchy, grieving, hideously ugly dog underfoot.

"That her kid?" he asked Donna.

She cast a quick look toward the booth where the girl was still engrossed in whatever she was reading. "Yeah. Fancy French name. *Gabrielle.* I told Becca the girl could spend an hour or so here before school starts, long as she behaves. This is her second morning here and she hasn't looked up from her book, not even to say thank-you when I fixed her a hot chocolate with extra whipped cream, on the house."

She seemed to take that as a personal affront and he had to smile. "Kids these days."

Donna narrowed her gaze at his cheek. "I'm just saying. Something's not right there."

"Order up," Lou called. "Chief's omelet's ready."

Donna headed back to the window and grabbed his breakfast and slid it expertly onto the counter. "You know where to find the salt and pepper and the salsa. But of course you won't need anything extra."

She headed off to take care of another customer and he dug into his breakfast. In the mirror above the counter, he had a perfect view of the new waitress as she scrambled around the diner. In the time it took him to finish his breakfast, he saw her mess up two orders and pour regular instead of decaf in old Bob Whitley's cup despite his doctor's orders that he had to ease up on the real stuff.

Oddly, she seemed to be going out of her way to avoid even making eye contact with him, though he thought he did intercept a few furtive glances in his direction. He ought to introduce himself. It was the polite thing to do, not to mention that he liked to make sure new arrivals to his town knew the police chief was keeping an eye out. But he wasn't necessarily inclined to be friendly to someone who could let a relative die a lonely death with only his farty, bad-tempered dog for company.

Fate took the decision out of his hands a moment later when the waitress fumbled the tray she was using to bus the table just adjacent to him. A couple of juice glasses slid off the edge and shattered on the floor.

"Oh, drat," the waitress exclaimed under her breath. The wimpy swear word almost made him smile. Only because he was so damn tired, he told himself.

On impulse, he unfolded himself from the barstool. "Need a hand?" he asked.

"Thank you! I…" She lifted her gaze from the floor to his jeans and then raised her eyes. When she identified him her hazel eyes turned from grateful to unfriendly and cold, as if he'd somehow thrown the glasses at her head.

He also thought he saw a glimmer of panic in those interesting depths, which instantly stirred his curiosity like cream swirling through coffee.

"I've got it, Officer. Thank you." Her voice was several degrees colder than the whirl of sleet outside the windows.

Despite her protests, he knelt down beside her and began to pick up shards of broken glass. "No problem. Those trays can be slippery."

This close, he picked up the scent of her, something fresh and flowery that made him think of a mountain meadow on a July afternoon. She had a soft, lush mouth and for one brief, insane moment, he wanted to push aside that stray lock of hair slipping from her ponytail and taste her. Apparently he needed to spend a lot less time working and a great deal more time recreating with the opposite sex if he could have sudden random fantasies about a woman he wasn't even inclined to like, pretty or not.

"I'm Trace Bowman. You must be new in town."

She didn't answer immediately and he could almost see the wheels turning in her head. Why the hesitancy? And why that little hint of unease he could see clouding the edges of her gaze? His presence was obviously making her uncomfortable and Trace couldn't help wondering why.

"Yes. We've been here a few weeks," she finally answered.

"I understand your grandfather was Wally Taylor."

"Apparently." She spoke in a voice as terse and cool as the freezing rain.

"Old Wally was an interesting guy. Kept to himself, mostly, but I liked him. You could always count on Wally not to pull any punches. If he had an opinion about something, you found out about it."

"I wouldn't know." She avoided his gaze, her voice low. He angled his head, wondering if he imagined sudden sadness in her eyes. What was the story here? He thought he remembered hearing years ago that Wally had been estranged from his only son. If that was the case, Trace supposed it wasn't really fair to blame the son's daughter for not maintaining a relationship with the old codger.

Maybe he shouldn't be so quick to judge the woman

until he knew her side of things. Until he had reason to think otherwise, he should be as friendly to her as he would be to anyone else new in his town.

"Well, I'm just up the road about four lots, in the white house with the cedar shake roof, if you or your daughter need help with anything."

She flashed a quick look toward the girl, still engrossed in her book. "Thank you. Very neighborly of you, Chief. I'll keep that in mind. And thank you for your help with my mess. Eventually I hope to stop feeling like an idiot here."

"You're welcome." He smiled as he picked up the last shard of glass and set it on her tray.

She didn't return his smile but he wanted to think she had lost a little of her wariness as she hurried away to take care of her tray and pick up another order from Lou at the grill window.

Definitely a story there. He just might need to dig a little into her background to find out why someone with fine clothes and nice jewelry who so obviously didn't have experience as a waitress would be here slinging hash at The Gulch. Was she running away from someone? A bad marriage? An abusive husband?

Now that the holidays were in full swing, the uptick in domestic-disturbance calls made that sort of thing a logical possibility. He didn't like to think about it. That young girl looked too bright and innocent to have to face such ugliness in her life. So did the mother, for that matter.

Rebecca Parsons. Becca. Not Becky. An intriguing woman. It had been a long time since one of those had crossed his path here in Pine Gulch.

He sipped at his juice and watched her deliver the

plate of eggs and bacon to Jolene Marlow. A moment later she was back at the window, telling Lou apologetically that the customer had asked for sausage and she hadn't written it down.

"She ever done this before?" Trace asked Donna with a jerk of his head toward Becca, as the other woman passed by on her way to refill another customer's cup.

Donna sighed. "I don't think so. I'm sure she'll pick up on it a little better any minute now." She frowned at him. "Don't you be giving her a hard time, pullin' your 'I'm just looking out for my town' routine. I get the feeling she's had a rough go of things lately."

"What makes you think?"

Donna cast a look to make sure Becca and the girl were both out of earshot before she lowered her voice. "She came in here three days ago practically begging for a job. Said she just needed something to tide her over for a few weeks and asked if she could work over the holidays for us. Smart girl knew to hit Lou up for the job instead of me. She must have seen he was the softy around here."

Trace decided he would be wise to keep his mouth shut about his opinions on that particular topic. Donna probably didn't need reminding about all the free meals she gave out to anyone who looked down on his luck or the vast quantities of food she regularly donated to the senior-citizens center for their weekly luncheons.

"Just be nice to her, okay? You were friendly with Wally, about the only one in town who could say that."

"He died alone with only that butt-ugly dog for company. Where was this granddaughter?"

Donna patted his shoulder in a comforting sort of way, giving her raspy smoker's cough. "I know Wally and his boy had a terrible falling-out years ago. You can't blame the granddaughter for that. If Wally blamed the girl for not visiting him, he never would have left his house to her, don't you think?"

Donna was right, damn it, as she so often was. He supposed he really would have to be a good neighbor to her and not just give lip service to the phrase.

That particular term made him think about her lips once more, lush and full and very kissable. He gave an inward groan. He really needed to go home and get some sleep if he was going to sit here and fantasize about a woman who might very well be married, for all he knew.

The chief of police. Just what she needed.

Becca hurried from table to table, refilling coffee and water, taking away plates, doing every busywork she could think of so she wouldn't have to interact with the gorgeous man who passed for the Pine Gulch long arm of the law.

It didn't seem right somehow. Why couldn't Trace Bowman be some kind of stereotype of a fat old guy with a paunch and a leering eye and a toothpick sticking out of the corner of his mouth? Instead he was much younger than she might have expected the chief of police to be, perhaps only mid-thirties. With brown hair and those piercing green eyes and a slow heartbreaker of a smile, he was masculine and tough and very, very dangerous, at least to her.

She should *not* have this little sizzle of awareness pulsing through her every time she risked another look at him. Police. Chief. Did she need any other reason to stay far, far away from Trace Bowman?

With habits ingrained from childhood, she cata-
logued all she had picked up about him from their brief
encounter. He either worked or played hard, judging
by the slight red streaks in his eyes, the circles under
them and the general air of fatigue that seemed to weigh
down his shoulders. Since he was still in uniform and
his boots were mud-splattered, she was willing to bet
it was the former.

He probably wasn't married—or at least he didn't
wear a wedding ring. She was voting on single status
for Pine Gulch's finest. If he had a wife, wouldn't it be
logical he'd be going home for a home-cooked breakfast and maybe a quickie after a long night instead of
coming into the diner? It was always possible he had
a wife who was a professional and too busy to arrange
her schedule around her husband's, but he gave off a
definite unmarried vibe.

He didn't seem particularly inclined to like her. She
might have wondered why not if he hadn't made that
comment about being her grandfather's neighbor. He
apparently thought she should have visited more. She
wanted to tell him how impossible that would have been
since she'd never even *heard* of Wally Taylor until she
received the notification of his death and his shocking
bequest, right when her own life in Arizona had been
imploding around her.

A customer asked her a question about the breakfast special, distracting her from thoughts of the police chief, and she forced herself to smile politely and
answer as best she could. As she did she was aware of
Trace Bowman standing up from the counter and tossing a few bills next to his plate, then shoving his hat on
and heading out into the cold drizzle.

The minute he left, she took her first deep breath since she'd looked up and seen the uniform walking into The Gulch.

The man didn't particularly like her and she had the vague sense that he was suspicious of her. Again, *not* what she needed right now.

She hadn't done anything wrong, she reminded herself. Not really. Oh, maybe she hadn't been completely honest with the school district about Gabi's identity but she hadn't had any other choice, had she?

Even knowing she had no reason to be nervous, law enforcement personnel still freaked her out. Old, old habit. Savvy civil servants ranked just about last on her mother's list of desirable associates. Becca would be wise to follow her mother's example and stay as far away from Trace Bowman as possible.

Too bad for her, he lived not far from her grandfather's house.

She glanced at her watch—one of the few pieces of jewelry she hadn't pawned—and winced. Once again, time was slipping away. She felt as if she'd been on her feet for days when it had been only an hour and a half.

She rushed over to Gabrielle, engrossed in reading *To Kill a Mockingbird,* a book Becca would have thought was entirely too mature for her except she'd read it herself at around that age.

"It's almost eight. You probably need to head over to the school."

Her half sister looked up, her eyes slightly unfocused, then released a heavy sigh and closed her book. "For the record, I still don't think it's fair."

"Yeah, yeah. I know. You hate it here and think the school is lame and well below your capabilities."

"It's a complete waste of my time. I can learn better on my own, just like I've always done."

Gabi was eerily smart for her age. Becca had no idea how she'd managed so well all these years when her education seemed to have been haphazard at best. "You've done a great job in school so far, honey. You're ahead of grade level in every subject. But for now school is our best option. This way you can make friends and participate in things like music and art. Plus, you don't have to be by yourself—and I don't have to pay a sitter—while I'm working."

They had been through this discussion before. Her arguments still didn't seem to convince Gabi.

"I can find her, you know."

She gave a careful look around to make sure they weren't being overheard. "And then what? If she'd wanted you with her, she wouldn't have left you with me."

"She was going to come back. How is she supposed to find us now, when you moved us clear across the country?"

Moving from Arizona to eastern Idaho wasn't exactly across the country, but she imagined it seemed far enough to a nine-year-old. She also wasn't sure what other choice she'd been given because of the hand Monica had dealt her.

"Look, Gab, we don't have time to talk about this right now. You have to head to school and I have to return to my customers. I told you that if we haven't heard from her by the time the holidays are over, we'll try to track her down, right?"

"That's what you *said*."

The girl didn't need to finish the sentence for Becca

to clearly understand. Gabrielle had spent nine years full of disappointments and empty promises. How could Becca blame her for being slow to trust that her sister, at least, meant what she said?

"We're doing okay, aren't we? School's not so bad, right?"

Gabi slid out of the booth. "Sure. It's perfect if you want me to be bored to death."

"Just hide your book inside your textbook," Becca advised. It had always worked for her, anyway, during her own slapdash education.

With a put-upon sigh, Gabi stashed her book into her backpack, slipped into her coat and then trudged out into the rain, lifting the flowered umbrella Becca had given her.

She would have liked to drive her sister the two blocks to school but she didn't feel she could ask for fifteen minutes off during the busiest time of the morning, especially when the Archuletas had basically done her a huge favor to hire her in the first place.

As she bused a table by the front window, she kept an eye on her sister. Between the umbrella and the red boots, the girl made a bright and incongruously cheerful sight in the gray muck.

She had no idea what she was doing with Gabi. Two months after she'd first learned she had a sister after a dozen years of estrangement from her mother, she wasn't any closer to figuring out the girl. She was brash and bossy sometimes, introspective and moody at others. Instead of feeling hurt and betrayed after Monica had dumped her on Becca, the girl refused to give up hope that her mother would come back.

Becca was angry enough at Monica for both of them.

Two months ago she'd thought she had her life completely figured out. She owned her own town house in Scottsdale. She had a job she loved as a real-estate attorney, she had a wide circle of friends, she'd been dating another attorney for several months and thought they were heading toward a commitment. Through hard work and sacrifice, she had carved her own niche in life, with all the safety and security she had craved so desperately when she was Gabi's age, being yanked hither and yon with a capricious, irresponsible con artist for a mother.

Then came that fateful September day when Monica had tumbled back into her life after a decade, like a noxious weed blown across the desert.

"Order up," Lou called from the kitchen. She jerked away from the window to the reality of her life now. No money, her career in tatters, just an inch or two away from being disbarred. The man she'd been dating had decided her personal troubles were too much of a liability to his own career and had dumped her without a backward glance, she had been forced to sell her town house to clean up Monica's mess, and now she was stuck in a sleepy little town in southeastern Idaho, saddled with responsibilities she didn't want and a nine-year-old girl who wanted to be anywhere else but here.

Any minute now, somebody was probably going to write a crappy country music song about her life.

To make matters even more enjoyable, now she'd raised the hackles of the local law enforcement. She sighed as she picked up the specials from Lou. Her life couldn't get much worse, right?

Even if Trace Bowman was the most gorgeous man she'd seen in a long, long time, she was going to have to do her best to keep a polite distance from the man. For now, she and Gabi had a place to live and the tips and small paycheck she was earning from this job would be enough to cover the groceries and keep the electricity turned on.

They were hanging by a thread and Chief Bowman seemed just the sort to come along with a big old pair of scissors and snip that right in half.

Chapter Two

Trace leaned back in his chair and set his napkin beside his now-empty plate. "Delicious dinner, Caidy, as always. The roast was particularly fine."

His younger sister smiled, her eyes a translucent blue in the late-afternoon November light streaming through the dining room windows. "Thanks. I tried a new recipe for the spice rub. It uses sage and rosemary and a touch of paprika."

"You know sage in recipes doesn't really come from the sagebrushes out back, right?"

She made a face at the teasing comment from Trace's twin brother, Taft. "Of course I know it's not the same. Just for that, you get to wash *and* dry the dishes."

"Come on. Have a little pity. I've been working all night."

"You were on duty," Trace corrected. "But did you

go out on any actual calls or did you spend the night bunking at the firehouse?"

"That's not the point," Taft said, a self-righteous note in his voice. "Whether I was sleeping or not, I was *ready* if my community needed me."

The overnight demands of their respective jobs had long been a source of good-natured ribbing between the two of them. When Trace worked the night shift, he was out on patrol, responding to calls, taking care of paperwork at the police station. As chief of the Pine Gulch fire department and one of the few actual full-time employees in the mostly volunteer department, Taft's job could sometimes be quiet.

They might bicker about it, but Trace knew no other person would have his back like his twin—though Caidy and their older brother, Ridge, would be close behind.

"Cut it out, you two." Ridge, the de facto patriarch of the family, gave them both a stern look that reminded Trace remarkably of their father. "You're going to ruin this delicious dessert Destry made."

"It's only boysenberry cobbler," his daughter piped in. "It wasn't hard at all."

"Well, it tastes like it was hard," Taft said with a grin. "That's the important thing."

Dinner at the family ranch, the River Bow, was a heralded tradition. No matter how busy they might be during the week with their respective lives and careers, the Bowman siblings tried to at least gather on Sundays when they could.

If not for Caidy, these Sunday dinners would probably have died long ago, another victim of their parents' brutal murders. For a few years after that fateful time a decade ago, the tradition had faded as Trace and his siblings struggled in their own ways to cope with their overwhelming grief.

Right around the time Ridge's wife left him and Caidy graduated from high school and started taking over caring for the ranch house and for Destry, his sister had revived the traditional Sunday dinners. Over the years it had become a way for them all to stay connected despite the hectic pace of their lives. He cherished these dinners, squabbles and all.

"I worked all night, too, but I'm not such a wimp that I can't take care of my fair share," he said with a sanctimonious look at his brother. "You sit here and rest, Taft. I wouldn't want you to overdo. I'll take care of the dishes."

Of course his brother couldn't let that insult stand, just as Trace expected. As a result, Taft became the designated dishwasher and Trace dried and put away the dishes while Destry and Ridge cleared the table.

Taft was just running water in the sink when Destry came in on her father's heels, her eyes as huge and plaintive as one of Caidy's rescued mutts begging for a treat. "Please, Dad. If we wait much longer, it will be too late."

"Too late for what?" Taft asked innocently.

"Christmas!" Destry exclaimed. "It's already the last Sunday in November. If we don't cut down our tree soon, the mountains will be too snowy. Please, Dad? Please, please, please?"

Ridge heaved a sigh. He didn't need to express his reluctance for Trace to understand it. None of his siblings had been very crazy about Christmas for nearly a decade, since their parents were killed just before Christmas Eve ten years ago.

"We'll get one," his brother assured Destry.

"What's the point of even putting up a tree if we wait much longer? Christmas will be over."

"It's not even December yet!"

"It's *almost* December. It will be here before we know it."

"She sounds like Mom," Taft said. "Remember how she used to start hounding Dad to cut the tree a few weeks before Thanksgiving?"

"And she always had it picked out by the middle of the summer," Caidy answered with a sad little smile.

"Please, Daddy. Can we go?"

Trace had to smile at his niece's persistence. Destry was a sharp little thing. She was generally a happy kid, which he found quite amazing considering her mother was a major bitch who had left Ridge and Destry when the little girl was still just a toddler.

"I guess you're right." Ridge eyed his brothers. "Either of you boys up for a ride to help me bring back the tree? We can get one for your places, too."

Taft shrugged. "I've got a date. Sorry."

"You have a date on a Sunday afternoon?" Caidy asked with raised eyebrows.

His brother seemed to find every available female between the ages of twenty-two and forty. "Not really a date. I'm going over to a friend's house to watch a movie and order pizza."

"You just had dinner," Caidy pointed out.

Taft grinned. "That's the thing about food...and other things. No matter how good the feast, you're always ready for more in a few hours."

"How old are you? Sixteen?" Ridge asked with a roll of his eyes.

"Old enough to thoroughly enjoy my pizza and everything that goes along with it," Taft said with another grin. "But you boys have fun cutting down your Christmas trees."

"You in?" Ridge asked Trace.

Since he didn't have a pizza buddy right now—or any other kind of euphemistically termed acquaintance—Trace figured he might as well. "Sure. I'm up for a ride. Let's go find a tree."

He could use a ride into the mountains. It might help clear the cobwebs out of his head from a week of double shifts.

The decision had been a good one, he decided a half hour later as he rode his favorite buckskin mare, Genie, up the trail leading to the evergreen forest above the ranch. He had needed to get out into the mountains on horseback again. The demands of his job as head honcho in an overworked and underfunded police department often left him with too little leisure time. He ought to make more time for himself, though. Right now, with feathery snowflakes drifting down and the air smelling crisp and clean, he wouldn't want to be anywhere else.

He loved River Bow Ranch. This was home, despite the bad memories and their grim past. Counting Destry now, five generations of Bowmans had made their home here, starting just after World War I with his great-grandfather. It was a lovely spot, named not only for the family name but also for the oxbow in Cold Creek that was a beautiful nesting spot in the summer for geese and swans.

Below the ranch, he could see the lights of Pine

Gulch gleaming in the dusk. His town. Yeah, it might sound like something out of an old Western, but he loved this little slice of western heaven. He'd had offers from bigger departments around Idaho and even a couple out of state. A few of them were tempting, he couldn't deny that. But every time he thought about leaving Pine Gulch, he thought about all the things he would have to give up. His family, his heritage, the comfort of small traditions like breakfast at The Gulch after an overnight shift. The sacrifices seemed too great.

"Thanks for coming with us," Destry said, reining her tough little paint pony next to his mare.

"My pleasure. Thanks for asking me, kid." His niece was turning into a good rider. Ridge had set her on the back of a horse from just about the moment she could walk and it showed. She had a confident seat, an easy grace, that had already won her some junior rodeo competitions.

"Are you finally going to put up a tree this year, Uncle Trace?"

"I don't know. Seems like a lot of trouble when it's only me."

He hated admitting that but it was true. He was tired of being alone. A year ago, he thought he was ready to settle down. He'd even started dating Easton Springhill. From here, he could see across the canyon and up to where she ran her family's place, Winder Ranch.

Easton wasn't for him. Some part of him had known it even as he'd tried to convince himself otherwise. Just *how* wrong she'd been for him had become abundantly clear when Cisco Del Norte came back to town and he saw for himself just how much Easton loved the man.

The two of them were deliriously happy now. They

had adopted a little girl, who was just about the cutest thing he'd ever seen, all big eyes and curly black hair and dimples, and Easton was expecting a baby in the spring. While Trace still wasn't crazy about Cisco, he had to admit the guy made Easton happy.

He had tried to convince himself he was in love with Easton but he recognized now that effort had been mostly based on hope. Oh, he probably could have fallen in love with her if he'd given a little more effort to it. Easton was great—warm and compassionate and certainly beautiful enough. They could have made a good life together here, but theirs would never have been the fierce passion she shared with Cisco.

A passion he couldn't help envying.

Maybe he would always be the bachelor uncle. It wasn't necessarily a bad role in life, he thought as Destry urged her pony faster on the trail.

"Almost there!" she exclaimed, her face beaming.

A few moments later they reached the thickly forested border of the ranch. Destry was quick to lead the way to the tree she had picked out months ago and marked with an orange plastic ribbon, just as their mother used to do.

Ridge cut the tree quickly with his chain saw while Destry looked on with glee. Caidy and a couple of her dogs had come up, as well—Trace had left Grunt, the ugly little French bulldog he'd inherited from Wally Taylor, back at the ranch house since the dog couldn't have kept up with the horses on his stubby little legs.

His sister didn't help cut down the tree, only stood on the outskirts of the forest, gazing down at town.

"How about you?" his brother asked. "You want us to cut one for you while we're up here?"

His brother asked every year and every year Trace gave the same answer. "Not much sense when it's just me. Especially since I'll be working through Christmas anyway."

Since he didn't have a family, he always tried to work overtime so his officers who did could have a little extra time off to spend with their children.

Caidy glanced over at them and he saw his own melancholy reflected in her eyes. Christmas was a hell of a time for the Bowman family. It probably always would be. He hated that she felt she had to hide away from life here with the horses and the dogs she trained.

"Hey, do you think we could cut an extra tree down for my friend?" Destry asked him.

"I don't mind. You'll have to ask your dad, though."

"Ask me what?" Ridge asked, busy tying the sled to his saddle for his horse to pull down the mountain.

"I wanted to give a tree to one of my friends."

"That shouldn't be a problem. We've got plenty of trees. But are you sure her family doesn't already have one?"

Destry shook her head. "She said they might not even put up a tree this year. They don't have very much money. They just moved to Pine Gulch and I don't think she likes it here very much."

Trace felt the same sort of tingle in his fingertips he always got when something was about to break on a case. "What's this friend's name?"

"Gabi. Well, Gabrielle. Gabrielle Parsons."

Of course. Somehow he'd known, even before Destry told him the name. He thought of the pretty, inept waitress with the secrets in her eyes and of the girl who had sat reading her book with such solemn concentration in the midst of the morning chaos at The Gulch.

"I met her the other day. She and her mother moved in near my house."

Both Ridge and Caidy gave him matching looks of curiosity and he shrugged. "She's apparently old Wally Taylor's granddaughter. He left the house to her, though I gather they didn't have much of a relationship."

"You really do know everything about what goes on in Pine Gulch," Caidy said with an admiring tone.

Trace tried his best to look humble. "I try. Actually, the mother is waitressing at The Gulch. I stopped there the other day for breakfast and ended up with the whole story from Donna."

"What you're saying, then," Ridge said, his voice dry, "is that *Donna* is the one in town who knows when every dog lifts his leg on a fire hydrant."

Trace grinned. "Yeah. So? A good police officer knows how to cultivate sources wherever he can find them."

"So can we cut a tree for Gabrielle and her mom?" Destry asked impatiently.

He remembered the secrets in the woman's eyes and her unease around him. He had thought about her several times in the few days since he saw her at the diner and his curiosity about why she had ended up in Pine Gulch hadn't abated whatsoever. He had promised himself he would try to be a good neighbor. What was more neighborly than delivering a Christmas tree?

"I don't see the problem with that. I can drop it off on my way home. Help me pick a good one for them."

Destry gave a jubilant cheer and grabbed his hand. "I saw the perfect one before. Come on, over here."

She dragged him about twenty feet away, stopping in front of a bushy blue spruce. "How about this one?"

The tree easily topped nine feet and was probably that big in circumference. Trace smiled at his niece's eagerness. "I'm sorry, hon, but if I remember correctly, I think that one is a little too big for the living room of their house. What about this nice one over here?" He led her to a seven-foot Scotch pine with a nice, natural Christmas-tree shape.

She gave the tree a considering sort of look. "I guess that would work."

"Here, you can help me cut it down then." He fired up Ridge's chain saw and guided his niece's hands. Together they cut the tree down and Trace tied it to his own horse's saddle.

"I hope Gabrielle will love it. You're going to take it to her tonight, right?" she demanded, proving once more that she was nothing like her selfish mother except in appearance. Destry was always thinking about other people and how she could help them, much like Trace's mother, the grandmother she had never met.

"I promise. But let's get it down the hill first, okay?"

"Okay." Destry smiled happily.

As they headed back toward River Bow Ranch while the sun finally slipped behind the western mountains, a completely ridiculous little bubble of excitement churned through him, like he was a kid waiting in line to see Santa Claus. He tried to tell himself he was only picking up on Destry's anticipation at doing a kind deed for her friend, but in his heart Trace knew there was more to it.

He wanted to see Becca Parsons again. Simple as that. The memory of her, slim and pretty and obviously uncomfortable around him, played in his head over and over. She was a mystery to him, that was all. He wanted only to get to know a few of her secrets and make sure she didn't intend to cause trouble in his town.

If anybody asked, that was his story and he was sticking to it.

Chapter Three

How did parents survive this homework battle day in and day out for *years?*

Becca drew in a deep, cleansing breath in a fierce effort to keep from growling in frustration at her sister and smoothed the worksheet out in front of them. They had only four more math problems and one would think she was asking Gabi to rip out her eyelashes one by one instead of just finish a little long division.

"We're almost done, Gab. Come on. You can do it."

"Of course I *can* do it." Though she was a foot and a half shorter than Becca, Gabi still somehow managed to look down her nose at her. "I just don't see why I have to."

"Because it's your homework, honey, that's why." Becca tried valiantly for patience. "If you don't finish it, you'll receive a failing grade in math."

"And?"

Becca curled her fingers into fists. Her sister was ferociously bright but had zero motivation, something Becca found frustrating beyond belief considering how very hard she had worked at school, the brief times she had been enrolled. In those days, she would rather have been the one ripping out her eyelashes herself rather than miss an assignment.

Not that her overachieving ways and conscientious study habits had gotten her very far.

She gazed around at the small, dingy house with its old-fashioned wallpaper and the water stains on the ceiling. She had a sudden memory of her elegant town house in an exclusive gated Scottsdale community, trim and neat with its chili-pepper-red door and the matching potted yucca plants fronting the entry. She suddenly missed her house with a longing that bordered on desperation. She would never have that place back. Her mother had effectively taken it from her, just like she'd taken so many other things.

She pushed away her bitterness. She had made her own choices. No one had forced her to sell her town house and use the equity to pay back her mother's fraud victims. She could have taken her chances that she might have been able to slither out of the mess Monica had left her with her career—if not her reputation— intact.

Again, not the issue here. She was as bad as Gabi, letting her mind wander over paths she could no longer change.

"If you flunk out of fourth grade, my darling sister, I'll have to homeschool you and we both know I'll be much tougher on you than any public school teacher. Come on. Four more questions."

Gabi gave a heavy sigh and picked up her pencil again, apparently tired of pitting her formidable will against Becca's. She finished the problems without any noticeable effort and then set down her pencil.

"There. Are you happy now?"

As Becca expected, her sister finished the problems perfectly. "See, that wasn't so tough, now, was it?"

Gabi opened her mouth to answer but before she could get the words out, the doorbell rang, making them both jump. The sudden hope that leapt into Gabi's eyes broke Becca's heart. She wanted to hug her, tell her all over again that Monica wasn't likely to come back.

"I'll get it," the girl said quickly, and disregarding all Becca's strictures about basic safety precautions, she flung open the door.

If ever a girl needed to heed stranger danger, it was now, Becca thought with a spurt of panic at the sight of the Pine Gulch chief of police standing on her doorstep. Trace Bowman looked dark and dangerous in the twilight and all her self-protective instincts ramped up into high gear.

Gabi looked disappointed for only a moment before she hid her emotions behind impassivity and eased away from the door to let Becca take the lead.

"Chief Bowman," she finally murmured. "This is... unexpected."

Not to mention unfortunate, unwelcome, unwanted.

"I know. Sorry to barge in like this but I've been charged with an important mission."

She glanced at Gabi and saw a flicker of curiosity in her sister's eyes.

The police chief seemed to be concealing something

out of sight of the doorway but she couldn't tell what it was from this angle.

"What sort of mission?" Becca was unsuccessful in keeping her wariness from her voice.

"Well, funny story. My niece, Destry, apparently is in the same school class as your daughter."

She couldn't correct his misstatement since she was the one who had perpetrated the lie. She shot a quick look at Gabi, willing her to keep her mouth shut. At the same time, she realized how rude she must appear to the police chief, keeping him standing on the sagging porch. She ought to invite him inside but she really didn't want him in her space. On the porch was still too close.

"Yes, Gabi's mentioned Destry."

"She's a great kid. Always concerned about those she counts as friends."

And he was telling her this why, exactly? She smiled politely, hoping he would get to the point and then ride off into the sunset on his trusty steed. Or maybe that pickup truck she could see parked in the driveway.

To her surprise, he appeared slightly uncomfortable. She thought she detected a hint of color on his cheekbones and he cleared his throat before he spoke again. "Anyway, Destry said Gabrielle told her you didn't have a Christmas tree yet and your daughter didn't know if you'd be putting one up this year."

She narrowed her gaze at Gabi, who returned the look with an innocent look. They had talked about putting a tree up. She'd promised her sister they would find something after payday the next week. She had to wonder if the concern from Chief Bowman's niece was spontaneous or if Gabi had somehow planted the seed somewhere.

"I'm sure we'll get something. We just…between moving in and settling into school and work, we haven't had much free time for, um, holiday decorating. It's not even December yet."

"I tried to tell Destry that but when we went up into the mountains this afternoon to find a tree for the ranch house, she had her heart set on cutting one for you, too. Look at it this way. One less thing you have to worry about, right?"

Finally he moved the arm concealed around the door-jamb so she could see that he was indeed holding a Christmas tree, dark green and fragrant.

"You don't get any fresher than this one. We just cut it about an hour ago."

A tree? From the chief of police? What kind of town was this?

She hadn't put up a Christmas tree in, well, ever. It had seemed far too much trouble when she was living alone. Besides, she had never had all that much to celebrate, busy with clients and contracts and court filings.

For an instant, she was transported to her very best memory of Christmas, when she was seven or eight and Monica had been working to empty the bank account of a lonely widower who had either been genuinely fond of Becca or had been very good at pretending. He had filled his house with Christmas decorations and presents. A wreath on the door, stockings hanging on the mantel, the whole bit.

She had really liked the old guy—until he'd called the police on Monica when he began to suspect she was stealing from them, and Becca and her mother had had to flee just a few steps from the law.

Now here was the chief of police standing on her doorstep with this lovely, sweet-smelling Christmas tree. "I...oh."

She didn't know what to say and her obvious discomfort must have begun to communicate itself to Trace Bowman.

"I can find another home for it if you don't want it," he finally said as the pause lengthened.

"Oh, please." Gabrielle clasped her hands together at her heart as if she were starring in some cheesy melodrama and trying desperately to avoid being tied to the railroad tracks by some dastardly villain. It was completely an act. *The part of Pleading Young Girl will be played tonight by the incomparable Gabrielle Parsons.*

Becca had no choice but to give in with as much grace as she could muster. And then figure out how she was going to afford lights and ornaments for the dratted thing.

"A tree would be lovely, I'm sure. Thank you very much." She *was* grateful. Her half sister might have the soul of a thirty-year-old con artist in a nine-year-old's body, but she was still a child. She deserved whatever poor similitude of Christmas Becca could manage.

"I didn't know if you would have a tree stand so I snagged a spare from the ranch house. If you'll just let me know where you want it, I can set this baby up for you."

"That's not necessary. I'm sure I can figure it out."

"Have you ever set a real tree up before?"

Real or fake, she didn't know the first thing about

a Christmas tree. Honesty compelled her to shake her head.

"It's harder than it looks. Consider the setup all part of the service."

He didn't wait for her to give him permission; he just carried the tree through the door and into her living room, bringing that sweet, wintry-tart smell and memories of happier times she had nearly forgotten.

"It's beautiful," Gabi exclaimed. "I think that might be the most beautiful tree I've ever seen."

Becca studied her sister. She couldn't say she'd figured out all her moods yet, but Gabi certainly looked sincere in her delight. Her eyes shone with excitement, her face bright and as happy as she'd seen it yet over the last two months. Maybe Becca was entirely too cynical. It was Christmas. Gabi had a right to her excitement.

"It really is a pretty tree," she agreed. "Where would you like Chief Bowman to put it, kiddo?"

"Right there facing the front window, then everyone will see it."

Gabi was full of surprises tonight. She usually preferred to stay inconspicuous to avoid drawing attention to herself. Becca had been the same way, trained well by a mother who was always just a pace or two ahead of the law.

Trace carried the tree over to the window and positioned it. The tree fit perfectly in the space, exactly the right height, as if he'd measured it.

"Right here?" he asked, his attention focused on Gabi.

"Maybe a little more to the left."

With a slightly amused expression, he moved the tree in that direction. When Gabi nodded he slanted a look at

Becca. She shrugged. Christmas tree positioning wasn't exactly in her skill set. Right along with waiting tables and trying to raise a precocious nine-year-old girl.

"Gabrielle, would you mind going back out onto porch for the tree stand I left there?" he asked. "I don't want to move from the perfect spot."

She hurried out eagerly and returned shortly with the green metal tree stand.

"Okay, I'm going to lift the tree and you set the stand with the hole right underneath the trunk. Got it?"

She nodded solemnly. When Trace effortlessly lifted the tree, she slid the stand where he indicated. Becca couldn't help but compare her eagerness to help Trace with the tree to her grave reluctance a few moments earlier to finish four measly math problems.

For the next few moments, Trace held the tree and instructed Gabi to tighten the bolts of the stand around the trunk in a particular order for the best stability.

Becca watched their efforts with a growing amusement that surprised her. She shouldn't be enjoying this. This was the police chief, she reminded herself, but it was hard to remember that when he was laughing with Gabi about the tree that seemed determined to list drunkenly to the side.

"I'm beginning to see why people prefer artificial trees."

"Oh, blasphemy!" He aimed a mock frown in her direction. "What about that heavenly smell?"

"A ninety-nine-cent car air freshener can give you the same thing without the sap and the needles all over the carpet."

He shook his head with a rueful smile but didn't argue and she was painfully aware of the highly inconvenient little simmer of attraction. He was an extraordinarily good-looking man, with those startling green eyes and a hint of afternoon shadow along his jawline. Avoiding him would be far easier if the dratted man didn't stir up all kinds of ridiculous feelings.

"I'll clean up the needles, I promise."

To Becca's surprise, Gabrielle seemed to glow with excitement. She was such a funny kid. Becca was no closer to figuring out this curious little stranger than she was two months ago when Monica had dumped her in her lap.

"Okay, moment of truth." Trace stepped back to look at his handiwork. "Does that look straight to you two?"

Gabrielle moved toward Becca for a better perspective and cocked her head to the side. "It looks great to me. What about you, Be—um, *Mom?*"

Gabi stumbled only slightly over the word but it was still a surprising mistake. Her sister was remarkably adept at deception. No surprise there since she'd been bottle-fed it since birth. Becca glanced at the police chief but he didn't seem to have noticed anything amiss and she spoke quickly to distract him.

"Looks straight to me, too."

"I think you're both right. It *is* straight. Amazing! That didn't take long at all. You've got some serious tree setup skills, young lady."

Much to Becca's astonishment, her sister giggled. Actually giggled. Gabrielle blinked a little, clearly surprised at the sound herself.

"Now what are we going to decorate it with?" the girl asked.

"I've got a couple strings of lights out in the truck. We can start with that."

"I can probably find something around here," Becca said quickly. "If not, I can pick some up tomorrow."

She didn't want him here. It was too dangerous. The more time they spent with the police chief, the greater the chance that either she or Gabi would slip again and he would figure out things weren't quite as they seemed. She had the distinct impression he was suspicious enough of them and she didn't want to raise any more red flags.

Her unwilling attraction to him only further complicated the situation. She just wanted him to leave so she could go back to duct-taping her life back together.

"I've already got the lights out in my truck. Why go to so much trouble of tracking down more?"

"You've already done more than enough."

"Here's something good to know about me." Trace grinned. "I'm the kind of guy who likes to see things through."

For an insane instant, she imagined just how he would kiss a woman—with thorough, meticulous intensity. Those green eyes would turn to smoke as he took great care to explore and taste every inch of her mouth with his until she was soft and pliant and ready to throw every caution out the window....

She blinked away the entirely too appealing image to find Trace watching her. His eyes weren't smoky now, only curious, as if wondering what she was thinking. Heat rushed to her cheeks with her blush, something she hadn't done in a long time. He wouldn't be talked out of helping them decorate the tree. Somehow she knew she was stuck in this untenable situation and continuing to protest would only make him wonder why she was so ardently determined to avoid his company.

Gabi was obviously pleased to have him here and it seemed churlish of Becca to make a deal about it. How long would it take to decorate a tree, anyway?

"Thank you, then. I think I saw a box of old ornaments up in the attic in my...my grandfather's things."

"Great. I guess we're in business." He headed for the door and returned a moment later with a box that had Extra Christmas Lights written on it with black permanent marker in what looked like a woman's handwriting. He didn't have a wife, she knew, so who had written those words? Maybe he had an ex or a steady girlfriend. Not that it was any of her business who might be writing on his boxes, she reminded herself.

He immediately started untangling the light strings and she watched long, well-formed fingers move nimbly for a moment then jerked her attention away when she realized she was staring.

"Gabi, come help me look for the ornaments."

Reluctance flitted across the girl's features as if she didn't want to leave Trace Bowman's presence, either, but she followed Becca up the narrow stairs to the cramped storage space under the eaves adjacent to the room Gabi had claimed as her own bedroom.

The space smelled musty and dusty and was piled with boxes and trunks Becca had barely had time to even look at in the few weeks they'd been in Pine Gulch. She pulled the string on the bare-bulb light and could swear she heard something scurry. They needed a cat, she thought. She didn't want to add one more responsibility to her plate but a good mouser would be just the thing.

"I think I saw the ornaments somewhere over by the window. Help me look, would you?"

She and Gabi began sorting through boxes filled with the detritus of a lonely old man's life. It made her inexpressibly sad to think about the grandfather she hadn't even known existed. Monica had told her very little about the paternal side of her heritage. She had known her father had died when she was just a baby and Monica had told her she didn't have any other living relatives on either side.

Big surprise. She'd lied. This was just one more thing her mother had stolen from her.

"He's nice, isn't he?"

She glanced at Gabi, who was looking toward the doorway and the stairs with a pensive sort of look.

"He's the police chief, Gab. You know what that means."

"We haven't done anything wrong here."

"Except tell the world I'm your mother."

She never should have done it, but it was one of those tiny lies that had quickly grown out of control. When she'd tried to enroll Gabi in school after they arrived in Pine Gulch, Becca had suddenly realized she didn't have any sort of guardianship papers or even a birth certificate. Worried that Gabi would be taken from her and placed into foster care, she had fudged the paperwork at the school. Thinking the school authorities would be more likely to take her word for things if she was Gabi's mother rather than merely an older sister, she had called upon the grifting skills she hadn't used in years to convince the secretary she didn't know where Gabi's birth certificate was after a succession of moves—not technically a lie.

The secretary had been gratifyingly understanding and told Becca merely to bring them when she could find them. From that moment, they were stuck in the lie. She didn't want to think about Trace Bowman's reaction if he found out she was perpetrating a fraud on the school and the community. She wasn't a poor single mother trying to eke out a living with her daughter. She was stuck in a situation that seemed to grow more complicated by the minute.

"I still think he's nice," Gabi said. "He brought us a Christmas tree."

She wanted to warn her sister to run far, far away from sexy men bearing warm smiles and unexpected charm. "You're right. That was a very kind thing to do. Actually, it was his niece's idea, right? You must have made a good friend in Destry Bowman."

"She's nice," Gabi said, avoiding her gaze. "Where do you think you saw the ornaments?"

An interesting reaction. She frowned at Gabi but didn't comment, especially when her sister found the box of ornaments just a moment later, next to a box of 1950s-era women's clothing.

Her grandmother's, perhaps? From the attorney who notified her of the bequest, she had learned the woman had died years ago, before she was born, but other than that she didn't know anything about her. Since coming to Pine Gulch, she had been thinking how surreal it was to live in her grandfather's house when she didn't know anything about him, surrounded by the personal belongings of a stranger.

She had picked up bits and pieces since she'd arrived in town that indicated that her father and grandfather had fought bitterly before she was born. She didn't know the full story and wasn't sure she ever would, but Donna told her that her father had apparently vowed never to speak to his own father again. She could guess the reason. Probably her mother had something to do with it. Monica was very good at finding ways to destroy relationships around her.

Kenneth Taylor had been killed in a motorcycle crash when Becca was a toddler and her parents had never been married. Her only memories of him were a bushy mustache and sideburns and a deep, warm voice telling her stories at night.

She'd been curious about her father's family over the years, but Monica had refused to talk about him. She hadn't even known her grandfather was still alive until she'd heard from that Idaho Falls attorney a few months earlier, right in the middle of her own legal trouble. When he had told her she had inherited a small house in Idaho, the news had seemed an answer to prayer. She had been thinking she and Gabi would wind up homeless if she couldn't figure something out and suddenly she had learned she owned a house in a town she'd never visited.

This sturdy little Craftsman cottage was dark and neglected, but she knew she could make a happy home here for her and Gabi, their lies notwithstanding.

As long as the police chief left her alone.

Females with secrets. He'd certainly seen his share of those.

Trace carefully wound the colored lights on the branches of their Christmas tree, listening to Becca and Gabi talk quietly as they pulled glass ornaments from a cardboard box. Something was not exactly as it appeared in this household. He couldn't put his finger on what precisely it might be but he'd caught more than one unreadable exchange of glances between Becca and her daughter, as if they were each warning the other to be careful with her words.

What secrets could they have? He had to wonder if they were on the run from something. A jealous ex? A custody dispute? That was the logical conclusion but not one that sat comfortably with him. He didn't like the idea that Becca might be breaking the law, or worse, in danger somehow. That would certainly make his attraction for her even more inconvenient.

He couldn't have said why he was still here. His plan when Destry had begged him to do this had been to merely do a quick drop-off of the tree, the stand and the lights. He'd intended to let Becca and Gabi deal with the tree while he headed down the street for a comfortable night of basketball in front of the big screen with his squash-faced little dog at his feet.

Instead, when he had shown up on the doorstep, she had looked so obviously taken aback—and touched, despite herself—that he had decided spending a little time with the two of them was more fascinating than even the most fierce battle on the hardwood.

He wasn't sorry. Gabi was a great kid. Smart and funny, with clever little observations about life. She, at least, had been thrilled by the donated Christmas tree, almost as if she'd never had a tree before. At some point, Gabi had tuned in on a Christmas station on a small boom box–type radio she brought from her bedroom. Though he still wasn't a big fan of the holiday, he couldn't deny there was something very appealing about working together on a quiet evening while snowflakes fluttered down outside and Nat King Cole's velvet voice filled the room.

It reminded him of happier memories when he was a kid, before the Christmas that had changed everything.

"That's the last of the lights. You ready to flip the switch?"

"Can I?" Gabi asked, her eyes bright.

"Sure thing."

She plugged in the lights and they reflected green and red and gold in her eyes. "It looks wonderful!"

"It really does," Becca agreed. "Thank you for your help."

Her words were another clear dismissal and he decided to ignore it. He wasn't quite ready to leave this warm room yet. "Now we can start putting up those ornaments."

She chewed her lip, clearly annoyed with him, but he only smiled and reached into the box for a couple of colored globes.

"So where were you before you moved to Pine Gulch?" he asked after a few moments of hanging ornaments. Though he pitted his question as casual curiosity, she didn't seem fooled.

Becca and her daughter exchanged another look and she waited a moment before answering. "Arizona," she finally said, her voice terse.

"Were you waitressing there?"

"No. I did a lot of different things," she said evasively. "What about you? How long have you been chief of police for the good people of Pine Gulch?"

He saw through her attempt to deflect his questions. He was fond of the same technique when he wanted to guide a particular discussion in an interview. He thought about calling her on it but decided to let her set the tone. This wasn't an interrogation, after all. Only a conversation.

"I've been on the force for about ten years, chief for the last three."

"You seem young for the job."

"I'm thirty-two. Not that young. You must have been a baby yourself when you had Gabi, right?"

He thought he saw a tiny flicker of something indefinable in the depths of her hazel eyes but she quickly concealed it. "Something like that. I was eighteen when she was born. What about you? Any wife and kiddos in the picture?"

Again the diversionary tactics. Interesting. "Nope. Never married. Just my brothers and a sister."

"And you all live close?"

"Right. My older brother runs the family ranch, the River Bow, just outside town. We run about six hundred head. My younger sister helps him around the ranch and with Destry. Then my twin brother, Taft, is the fire chief. You might have seen him around town. He's a little hard to miss since we're identical."

"Wow. There are two of you?"

"Nope. Only one. Taft is definitely his own man."

She smiled a little as she reached to hang an ornament on a higher branch. Her soft curves brushed his shoulder—completely accidental, he knew—and his stomach muscles contracted. He hadn't felt this little zing of attraction in a long, long time and he wanted to savor every moment of it, despite his better instincts reminding him he knew very little about the woman and what he did know didn't seem completely truthful.

She moved away to the other side of the tree and picked up a pearly white globe ornament from the box.

He thought her color was a little higher than it had been before but that could have been only the reflection from the Christmas lights.

"You haven't had the urge to explore distant pastures? See what's out there beyond Pine Gulch?"

"Been there, done that. I spent four years as a Marine MP, with tours in the Middle East, Germany, Japan. I was ready to be back home."

He didn't like to think about what had happened after he came home, restless and looking for trouble. He'd found it, far more than he ever imagined, in the form of a devious little liar named Lilah Bodine.

"And the small-town life appeals to you?"

"Pine Gulch is a nice place to live. You won't find a prettier place on earth in the summertime and people here watch out for each other."

"I'm not sure that's always a good thing, is it? Isn't that small-town code for snooping in other people's business?"

What in her past had made her so cynical? And what business did she have that made her eager to keep others out of it?

"That's one way of looking at it, I suppose. Some people find it a comfort to know they've always got someone to turn to when times are tough."

"I'm used to counting on myself."

Before he could respond to that, Gabi popped her head around the side of the Christmas tree, a small porcelain angel with filigree wings in her hand. "This was the last ornament in the box," she said. "Where should I put it?"

Becca looked at the tree. "Well, we don't have anything at the top. Why don't we put her there?"

"That seems about right," Trace said. "A tree as pretty as this one deserves to have an angel watching over it."

"Okay. I'll have to get a chair."

"Why?" He grinned at the girl and picked her up. She seemed skinny for her age and she giggled a little as he hefted her higher to reach the top of the tree. She tucked the little angel against the top branch and secured her with the clip attached to her back.

"Perfect," Gabi exclaimed when she was done.

He lowered her to the ground and the girl hurried to turn off the light switch to the overhead fixture and the two lamps until the room was dark except for the gleaming, colorful tree.

They all stepped back a little for a better look. Much to his surprise, as he stood in this dark, dingy little house with that soft music in the background and the snow drifting past the window and the tree lights flickering, he felt the first nudge of Christmas spirit he'd experienced in a long, long time.

"It's magical," Gabi breathed.

Becca leaned down and hugged her. "You know what, kiddo? *Magical* is exactly the right word."

They all stood still for a moment. Becca was the first to break the spell.

"I'm sorry we kept you so long." She smiled at him and he had the feeling it was the most genuine smile she'd ever given him. "You didn't need to stay to help us decorate the whole thing."

"You didn't see me rushing for the door, did you?" he answered. "I could have left anytime. If I hadn't been enjoying myself, I would have been gone. I don't usually get into Christmas, but this was fun."

She gave him a curious look, as if surprised that he could possibly enjoy something so tame as decorating a tree. He wasn't sure he could explain it to her when he didn't quite understand it himself.

"Would you like some cocoa?" she asked, and he had the vague impression the invitation hadn't been planned.

He was tempted by the offer, more tempted than he should have been, but he was beginning to think regaining a little distance between them would be smart.

"Another time, maybe. I've got an early day tomorrow. I dropped my dog off at home after we cut the tree down and I probably need to head back and put him out."

She nodded and walked him to the door, where he retrieved his parka from the hook by the door. "Well, thank you again," she said. "It really was a kind thing to do. Please tell your niece we appreciate it."

"I'll do that." He shrugged into his coat. He reached for the door handle, then completely on impulse, leaned in and kissed her cheek. She smelled delicious, sweetly female, and her skin was warm against his mouth.

It was a crazy gesture and totally unlike him and he had no idea what had compelled him. Must be some weird holiday insanity. When he drew away, she was staring at him, her eyes as huge as Gabi's had been when she first saw the tree.

"Good night," he said quickly and opened the door before she could respond.

What just happened there? he wondered as he climbed into his pickup for the half-block drive to his house. He really had planned to just drop off the tree and go. Instead, he had spent more than an hour helping her set up the tree and then decorate it. And then he had complicated matters by that ridiculous brush of his mouth on her cheek.

He felt sorry for the woman and her kid. That was all. She was obviously in a tight spot financially. She was alone in a new town without friends or family. He was only helping her out, doing just what any good neighbor would do.

He refused to think he allowed himself any other motive. He wasn't at all eager to throw his heart out there again—and if he did, he certainly wouldn't hand it over to a woman like Becca who was obviously hiding something from him. He'd learned his lesson about lying women.

Chapter Four

"Would any of you like a refill?" With the pot of decaf in one hand and the good stuff in the other, Becca smiled at The Gulch regulars, a group that had met there every single morning since she'd started working at the diner.

She had come to find great comfort in their consistency, listening to them bicker and joke around with each other and other restaurant patrons. Though they all apparently came from very different demographic and socioeconomic backgrounds, they seemed like a family, dysfunctions and all.

"Top me off, would you?" Mick Malone gestured to his cup and she was rather proud of herself for remembering he drank only decaf. She managed to pour his refill without spilling a drop, another mark of just how far she'd apparently come in the nearly two weeks since she'd started working at the diner.

"Another stack, Sal? I can have Lou throw a few more cakes on the griddle."

"This ought to hold me until lunch, darlin'."

She smiled at the older cowboy. He had to be in his seventies and so skinny he probably had trouble keeping his jeans up, but the guy had the metabolism of a hummingbird, apparently, and could eat every other one of the regulars under the table.

"Anyone else need anything?"

"I'll take one of those pretty smiles if you've got another one to spare." Jesse Redbear, missing his left front tooth, gave her a flirtatious grin that lifted all his wrinkles. She shook her head but couldn't resist a smile.

"That's the one." He winked at her. "I think I'm good now."

She shook her head again. "I'll check on you all again in a minute," she said, then moved to the other side of her section to check on a couple of customers who had just sat down.

She couldn't say she would be sorry to leave waitressing behind when she finished the requirements to transfer to the Idaho state bar, but she had certainly learned a lot the last few weeks working at The Gulch. She had learned that sometimes the stingiest-looking customers could be the biggest tippers, that keeping beverages topped off could go a long way and that sometimes a friendly, apologetic smile could make all but the most dour customers forgive her frequent mistakes.

"Order up," Lou called from the grill, and she finished taking the newcomers' orders then headed back to pick up the breakfast specials for a young family she'd seen around town before. When the bell chimed on the door, heralding a new arrival, she looked up just as everyone else did.

The chief of police walked in looking dark and gorgeous, and her stomach fluttered wildly, until she noticed the pretty ski-bunny type who came in with him, hanging on his arm as if she were a bounty hunter and he was prey about to escape.

They didn't take a table, just stood for a moment near the entrance. To Becca's dismay, he gave the woman a playful kiss and it was obvious they'd just spent the night together. Her stomach dived down to her feet and she thought of how stupid she'd been to have cherished that sweet little kiss on the cheek he'd given her nearly a week earlier when he'd come to help them with their Christmas tree.

"Come have a cup of coffee at least," he said in a low bedroom voice.

"I can't stay," the woman protested. "I'm already late for work. I'll see you later, though, right?"

"Plan on it." He kissed her again, and the ditzy-looking woman left the diner with a longing sort of backward glance.

Becca somehow wasn't surprised when he sat down in her section. Annoyed with herself for the completely unreasonable jealousy seething through her, she set the menu down in front of him with a little more brusqueness than normal. "Good morning, Chief. Do you want coffee this morning?"

She heard the coolness in her voice and he must have picked up on it, too, because he finally met her gaze with a surprised sort of look. Becca faltered. This wasn't Trace Bowman. It must be his twin, she realized with growing mortification.

"I'm so sorry. You're not Chief Bowman."

"Actually, I am. Just not the *only* Chief Bowman."

Trace's twin was the fire chief, she remembered belatedly. Now that she had a better look at him, she realized that while they were identical twins, there were definite differences. This Bowman was a little broader in the shoulders, his hair was a little shaggier and he didn't come across quite as dangerously masculine.

And apparently he was the ladies' man of the family. He gave her a charmer of a grin. "I'm the better-looking chief."

"I'm sorry. I forgot you were twins."

"I'm Taft Bowman, with the Pine Gulch Fire Department." He held out a hand to shake hers and she had no real choice but to reach out to return the gesture.

"I'm Rebecca Parsons."

"Right. You're new in town, Wally Taylor's granddaughter. You must be the one with the kid our Destry's age."

Our Destry. She had to admit, she was touched by his words, as if the entire Bowman clan seemed to take responsibility for the little girl. That sort of family unity was completely beyond anything in her experience.

"That's right." She gave him a smile she hoped was slightly warmer. "Do you need time to look at the menu or do you know what you want?"

This was another thing she'd learned in her few weeks working at The Gulch. Townsfolk generally already had their orders picked out before they ever walked through the doors.

"I'm in the mood for a ham-and-cheese omelet this morning. Think you can talk Lou into making one for me?"

Apparently Taft Bowman had enough experience with Lou that he knew he could sometimes be in a mood. "I'll certainly ask him. He's done a few other omelets this morning, so keep your fingers crossed. I think you should be safe."

His green eyes that seemed just like Trace's gleamed appreciatively as he smiled at her. He was every bit as good-looking as his brother and she wondered why his smile didn't stir her hormones in the slightest. She was as unmoved by his flirting as she had been to Jesse Redbear's.

Maybe it was because the fire chief was an obvious player, judging by the woman who had just left. But she had a feeling if Trace had looked at her that way, she would have dissolved into a puddle all over the peeled plank floor of The Gulch.

"The fire chief would like a ham-and-cheese omelet."

Lou frowned as he turned some sizzling bacon on the grill. "That can probably be arranged."

She realized after she gave the order that she'd forgotten to ask Trace's brother if he wanted coffee. By the time she turned back to remedy her mistake, he had swiveled around in his booth and was talking to a couple of middle-aged women at the next table, who simpered and blushed at his teasing.

She fought an amused smile as she headed back toward his booth. "Coffee, Chief?"

He aimed that flirtatious grin at her. "Thanks. Give me the high-octane stuff."

She had only started to pour when the door opened again and the *other* Chief Bowman walked inside. How could she ever have mistaken Taft for his brother? They weren't anything alike, she saw now. Her stomach gave a silly little swoop and she remembered again the soft brush of his mouth on her skin.

"Um. Ow."

She jerked her gaze away at the calm words and was horror-stricken to realize she had splashed hot coffee on the fire chief's leg.

"Oh. Oh! I'm so sorry. Let me just..." She pulled off the towel tucked into her apron and began dabbing at the spot. He eased back in the booth and gave her an amused look, and she was painfully aware of Trace walking toward their table. When he reached it, he stood there for a moment watching her dab at his brother's thigh before he cleared his throat.

"What have we here?"

"Just a little coffee mishap," his twin said. "No worries. It's probably not even a third-degree burn."

"I've been doing so well all morning," she wailed, then glared at Trace. "Why did you have to come in and ruin everything?"

Oh, she hadn't meant to say that. She was suddenly aware that both men were suddenly watching her with interest. Heat rushed to her face and she wanted to sink through the floor with mortification. Trace Bowman made her nervous and off balance and now everyone in the diner within earshot knew it.

She took a deep breath and pulled the towel away from the fire chief, praying for composure.

"I really am sorry," she said to him.

"I'm fine," he said again. "My Levi's took the brunt of it."

To her vast relief, Lou rang the bell in the window. "Order up," he called.

"That would be your omelet, Chief."

Trace, just sliding into the booth across from his brother, gave her a teasing smile. "How'd you know I was in the mood for an omelet?"

"Get your own. That one's mine." Taft gave him a mock scowl.

Trace raised an eyebrow with a meaningful look she didn't understand. "Funny. I was just going to say the same thing to you."

She didn't have time to figure out the subtext between them as she headed back toward the grill to pick up the order. Nor did she understand why, when faced with two equally gorgeous men, did only one of them seemed to possess the power to turn her into a babbling idiot?

"Here's the chief's omelet," Lou said. "Comes with a short stack."

"Thanks."

"What about the other chief?"

She let out a breath. She did *not* want to have to deal with the man this morning. "He said something about an omelet as well but I'll have to go check to make sure."

Lou refrained from rolling his eyes but he still looked faintly exasperated, probably wondering why she hadn't asked when she was just at the booth, but he didn't push her. Becca grabbed the eggs and pancakes and returned to the Bowman brothers' booth.

She slid the plates down in front of the fire chief, along with a small syrup container. At least she didn't spill that all over him, too.

"Anything else I can do for you?"

The fire chief opened his mouth, a teasing gleam in his green eyes, but then she heard a dull thud from under the table and his flirtatious expression shifted to one of almost pain. "I'm good. Really, really great. Thanks."

She looked suspiciously at Trace but he only smiled blandly.

"Are you ready to order?" she asked.

"I think I know what I want."

She reached into her apron pocket for her order pad and was happy her fingers trembled only a little when she gripped her pencil. "I'm ready. Go ahead."

"I changed my mind about the omelet. Think I'm in the mood for something sweet. I'll have the French toast. Oh, and a side of scrambled eggs. Thank you."

"Coffee?"

"Decaf."

She poured for him, focusing all her concentration on not spilling a single drop. After she finished giving his order to Lou, the large group at the corner booth next to the Bowman brothers left and she hurried over to bus their table. Though she didn't intend to eavesdrop on the conversation of Trace and his brother, she couldn't help overhearing a little of it as she cleared away plates.

"Any guesses what might be going on with her?" Taft asked the police chief.

"No. Something's up, though. I stopped by the ranch last night to drop off a book I'd borrowed from Caidy, and Destry stayed in her room the whole time."

"That's not like her." The easy charm of the fire chief faded into concern. "Wonder if she's sick."

Becca frowned as she wiped down the table with a clean cloth. She hoped not. Gabrielle seemed to be spending a lot of time with Trace's niece. If Destry got sick, chances were Gabi would get it, too. Becca couldn't afford to miss work to stay home with her sister if Gabi caught some nasty bug.

"Caidy said she seemed to be feeling fine. No fever or complaining about any symptoms of sore throat or stomachache or anything. She's just been really quiet and sad for a few days. Caidy said she's not eating much and she didn't want to go on a ride with her yesterday after school."

"That's *really* not like her."

"I talked to Caidy this morning and she said Destry refused to stay home, said she was fine. Caidy's worried about her, too."

She didn't hear the rest as she had finished clearing off the corner booth and had no excuse to linger here, especially when she had other customers with needs. For the next ten minutes, she did her best to ignore the Bowman brothers, though she was aware of them— okay, aware of *Trace*—as she took orders, seated new customers, poured coffee refills.

When Lou announced his order was ready, Becca ordered herself to be calm and collected. He was just another customer, she told herself as she set the fluffy eggs and cinnamon French toast on a tray.

She might have even believed it if her nerves didn't jump like crazy, simply from being this close to him.

"Thank you." His warm smile of appreciation didn't help matters whatsoever. She wanted to bask in that smile like a kitten in a sunbeam.

Becca quickly did her best to clamp down on the inappropriate response. She didn't need a man to further snarl up her life, especially when she seemed to be doing a fine job of that all on her own.

"More coffee?" she asked them.

Trace nodded and she refilled his cup first then used the other pot of regular to top off his brother's.

"Anyway, you know how Ridge can be," Taft said, obviously continuing the conversation between them. "If something doesn't moo or neigh, he doesn't pay it much attention."

"Hey, Becca. You live with a nine-year-old girl," Trace said suddenly.

"Yes," she said carefully.

"We're both a little concerned for our niece, Destry. She's been acting weird this week. Secretive, you know."

"It *is* almost Christmas. Maybe she's working on a special present."

"That's a possibility, but it's not reading that way to me," Trace said.

"She's usually the only one in the family who's excited about Christmas," Taft said. "Not this year, though. I offered to take her Christmas shopping over the weekend so we could get something for her dad and Caidy, and she shut me down right away."

"Why?"

"No idea," Trace answered. "That's what we were hoping you could shed some insight about. You being a girl and also being the mother to a girl the same age."

Her stomach twisted a little at the reminder of her lie and she could feel herself flush. "I meant, why doesn't more of your family enjoy Christmas?"

The two men exchanged a look, both suddenly solemn. "Memories," Trace finally said. "Our parents died around Christmastime. This year is the ten-year anniversary of their deaths."

She had known, somehow, that he carried a deep pain

around the holiday. When he had been at their house the other night helping with the tree, he had laughed and joked with them, but she had seen a shadow in his eyes a few times.

"I'm sorry," she said. "I shouldn't have pried. No wonder you want to avoid the holiday altogether."

"We might want to, but we understand that Destry's just a kid. Since she was little, we've all tried to put on a good show for her."

Again she was struck at the Bowman siblings' love and concern for the little girl. For a crazy moment, she was consumed with envy. She would have loved this sort of extended family when she was a child. Instead, all she'd had was Monica.

Gabrielle had more than that, she suddenly realized. Gabi had *her*. She could guess that her younger sister probably didn't have that many warm, cherished Christmas memories. Not with Monica raising her in the same haphazard way she had raised Becca. But Gabi had an older sister who could give her everything she had missed for the past nine years. Christmas carols and sleigh rides, home-baked cookies and stockings on the mantel.

She had been trying to merely survive the holidays until she found a little better footing, but Gabi deserved more than that. Like it or not, she needed to step up for her little sister's sake, just as the Bowmans tried to do for their niece.

"Any ideas what we can do for Des?" Taft asked.

They were asking the wrong person. She was just about the last one on earth with many insights into the mind of a nine-year-old girl. "You're going to have to figure out what's wrong first. What does she say when you ask?"

"Nothing," Trace said. "She says she's fine."

"I can ask my…Gabi if you'd like. They seem to be friends. If anyone can wiggle out the truth about what might be bothering Destry, it's Gabrielle."

"That would be great." Taft smiled at her and she wondered again at the capriciousness of fate. She had absolutely no reaction to his smile other than a pleasant warmth.

When she met Trace's glittery green gaze, that warmth exploded into a churning, seething firestorm, and she wanted to stand there and bask in the heat of it.

"Excuse me, miss? Can I get more water?"

At the voice from a neighboring table, Becca jerked her attention back to her job and the ten other tables full of customers who needed her. "Excuse me. I'm sorry."

She grabbed up the water pitcher and refilled the water glasses at the neighboring table, reminding herself as she attended to her other customers of all the reasons why fraternizing with local law enforcement was a bad idea.

She might not be running a con but she was definitely living a lie. If he found out the truth—that Gabi was her younger sister, not her daughter, and that Becca didn't have any kind of official custody arrangement with their mother—authorities could conceivably take the girl from her and put her into foster care. She couldn't let that happen to her sister.

The Bowman brothers seemed to be taking their time over their food and she tried not to pay any more attention to them than strictly necessary to make sure they had adequate service. The other customers kept her busy, especially the large group of college-age snow-mobilers, in town for the weekend, that ended up taking the corner booth near Trace and his brother.

They were demanding and petulant and becoming louder by the minute, to the point where she almost expected Lou to come out from behind the grill and start swinging his frying pan around.

They were also not nearly as respectful as the local customers. Their flirting with her had a hard edge to it and when she reached to refill one coffee cup, the young man on the end of the booth tried to cop a quick feel.

She instinctively squeaked and backed away. Before she'd even caught her breath, Trace was looming behind her. For a large man, he moved with deadly stealth, turning from amiable to dangerous in the space of a heartbeat.

He'd been a military policeman, she remembered him saying. She could quite clearly picture him knocking a couple of shaved marine heads together for disturbing the peace. He had the harsh, indestructible look of a leatherneck. Definitely not someone to mess around with.

"Thank you for breakfast, Becca." He barely looked at her when he spoke, his attention on the rough group of snowmobilers.

"You're welcome," she said. She could probably handle a group of kids on her own but she couldn't deny she was grateful to Trace for stepping in.

"You think you could top off my coffee one more time before I go?"

"Sure. Right away, Chief Bowman."

She quickly escaped the tension and returned to the neighboring booth, where she quickly refilled his coffee. Taft said something to her about the weather and she answered distractedly, her attention still focused on Trace, who had now bent down and murmured something to the college kids. She couldn't hear what he said but she saw the boy who had tried to grope her blanch as if he'd just driven his snowmobile into an icy lake.

He nodded vigorously and then all of the kids dug into their food while Trace moved leisurely back to his own booth.

She felt compelled to say something. "Thank you. I could have handled the situation, but…thank you."

"No problem. They shouldn't bother you again."

"Just out of curiosity, what did you use on the little punks?" the fire chief asked. "The line about how you keep the band castrator we use on the cattle in the back of your squad car and aren't afraid to use it?"

He gave a slow smile that ramped her heartbeat up a notch. "No, but that's always a good one. I just told them we have old-fashioned ideas around here about the way men ought to treat women. And that I have a special jail cell at the station house for little punks who come to town looking for trouble. They shouldn't bother you again. You let me know if they do."

"I will," she mumbled and moved quickly away before she did something completely ridiculous like burst into tears.

She was more shaken by the incident than she wanted to admit—more by her reaction to what Trace had done than by a stupid little punk trying for a cheap thrill.

Becca had been taking care of herself virtually since birth, since Monica had all the maternal instincts of a blowfly. Despite that, she had worked hard to become a competent, self-assured adult. She had been on her own since she became an emancipated minor at sixteen and had convinced herself she didn't need anyone.

So why did she literally go weak in the knees when a sexy police chief stepped up to watch over her?

She had no answer for that. She only knew she couldn't make up for the inadequacies of her childhood by seeking someone to watch over her as an adult. Right now her focus needed to be Gabi and nurturing her baby sister the way their mother never had.

Chapter Five

"I'm not going to stand for it, you hear me?" Ralph Ashton's face was florid, his eyes an angry, snapping brown. "I pay taxes in this town, have done for sixty-five years now. When I'm being robbed blind, I've got a right to expect the police to do more than stand around scratching their behinds."

Trace fought for patience as he stood in the narrow aisle of the store the man had owned for years. Like an old-fashioned general store, Ashton's sold everything from muck boots to margarine, pitchforks to potato chips. In his early eighties now, Ralph Ashton had been running the place since he was a teenager. He should have stepped down years ago but he still insisted he was perfectly competent to manage the day-to-day operations of the store, much to the frustration of his children—and the frustration of law enforcement officials who had to deal with his frequent complaints about shoplifters.

"You're absolutely right, Mr. Ashton. I'm sorry we haven't been able to figure out who's stealing candy bars out of your inventory. I still think it's probably kids pulling a prank, but maybe there's more to it."

"It's high time you did something about this. Set up a sting or something."

"If you would stop erasing your security film every twelve hours, I might have a better chance of figuring things out."

"You know how expensive that film is?"

They had had this argument often and Trace knew a losing cause when he stared it in the eye. He was about to respond when a new customer came into the store. His pulse jumped when he saw Becca Parsons pull a shopping cart out of the row and head off in the other direction.

Though it was a wintry December day with snow falling steadily, she was like a breath of springtime, like standing in a field of daffodils while birds flitted around him building nests....

The whimsy of that sudden image popping into his head left him unnerved and he quickly turned back to Mr. Ashton.

"If you want to catch the shoplifters, you might have to spend a little money to do it."

"I've spent money! I pay my taxes. I have rights, don't I? It's a disgrace. That's what it is. These rotten kids are bleeding me dry and you won't even dust for fingerprints. I'm calling the mayor. Right now. See if I don't."

The old man was growing increasingly agitated,

Trace saw with concern. He nodded in a placating sort of way. "I understand your frustration, Mr. Ashton. Honestly, I do. I'm sorry we haven't had more luck. Let's talk about our options. Why don't you sit down and take a rest? Where's Rosalie?" Ashton's grand-daughter usually did her best to take over as many store responsibilities as Ralph would let her.

"Useless thing. She took her mother to a doctor's ap-pointment in Idaho Falls. Seemed to think the assistant manager could run the place on his own." He spoke as if that was the most ridiculous idea he had ever heard, as if he were the only one fit to make decisions.

Trace didn't like Ralph Ashton—the guy had been a grumpy old cuss ever since he could remember—but he still had to respect the man's dedication to his busi-ness and he couldn't help the stirring of pity when he saw the tremble of Ralph's hands as he straightened a row of canned peaches on the shelf above them.

"Look, I'll fingerprint the rack if you'll agree to go sit down in Rosalie's office and work on some paper-work or something. The assistant manager can still find you if he needs help with anything."

"You're just trying to get rid of me and then you're going to duck out and leave me to deal with these lousy shoplifters on my own."

Trace gave him a stern look. "I said I'll check for fin-gerprints and I will. You can watch me the whole time through the security cameras. You know we Bowmans keep our word, Mr. Ashton."

Ralph gave him a considering look. "True enough. Your parents were good folks. I always used to say your dad was about the only honest man in town. If he said he would pay you in a few weeks, you'd get your money right on the dot."

The reminder of Trace's father seemed to convince the man. "I do have plenty of paperwork. Just let me know when you're done."

He stumped off, his cane making a staccato beat through the store. Trace gave a heavy sigh and turned back to the candy rack. This was a completely futile exercise when half the people in town bought gum and candy bars from Ashton's Mercantile, but he would keep his word and humor the guy. And then maybe he would have a good, long talk with Rosalie about increasing their security budget a little and maybe stationing a stocker nearby after school to keep a better eye out.

He was just lifting his eighth set of prints—for all he knew, it could have been his own since he'd bought a tin of wintergreen Altoids a few days earlier—when Becca turned onto his aisle, her shopping cart full of budget items like macaroni-and-cheese boxes and store-brand cereal. She did have some baking supplies—butter, sugar, flour, as well as some cake decorating sprinkles and colored icing—and he guessed Christmas cookies were in her immediate future.

When she spotted him, her eyes lit up with warmth but she quickly concealed her expression. He'd never known a woman so guarded with her emotions. What made her so careful? Was it something about him or did she have that reaction to everyone? He very much wanted to find out. He remembered his ridiculous imagery of earlier, how she seemed to bring springtime into the store with her despite the snow he could see through the front doors, which was now blowing harder than ever.

He found it more than a little unsettling how happy he was to see her or how many times in the last week since he last saw her that he had driven past her house at the end of a long shift and been tempted to turn into the driveway toward those glowing lights. He hadn't been this interested in a woman in a long time.

"How have you been? I haven't seen you in a while."

"You haven't been into The Gulch lately. At least not during my shift."

"I've stopped in a few times for dinner." *But you weren't there.* He decided it would be better to leave that particular disappointment unspoken.

"Lou and Donna have been really great to let me work mostly the breakfast and lunch crowds so I can be with Gabi after school and in the evenings."

"They're good that way."

She smiled. "That's exactly the word. They're *good.* Really nice people."

He raised an eyebrow. "You sound surprised."

"Not surprised, exactly. I'm just not…used to it, I guess. They've been extraordinarily kind to me."

"That's the way they are."

"I keep thinking how lucky I am that The Gulch was the first place I applied for a job when I came to town. I'm amazed they've let me stay, if you want the truth." She gave him a rueful smile. "I'm really not waitress material. You may have noticed."

"You're doing fine."

"I'm not, but I'm trying. I'm amazed at how patient and kind they've been with me. I keep looking for an ulterior motive but so far I can't find anything."

He wondered again at her life before she moved into her grandfather's house. What experience with the world led a woman to become so cynical that she constantly seemed braced for hurt and didn't know how to accept genuine kindness when it came her way?

"They don't have an ulterior motive, I can promise you. That's just who they are. Lou and Donna care about Pine Gulch and the people in it. You'll find when you've been around a little longer that this town is lucky enough to have more than a few people like the Archuletas. Good, honest, hardworking people who watch out for each other."

"I'm beginning to see that," she murmured. She made a vague gesture at the candy rack and his evidence bag open in front of him. "What are you doing?"

In light of the claim he'd just made about Pine Gulch and the town's inhabitants, he felt a little sheepish replying, "Okay, not everyone is honest. Ralph Ashton, who owns the store, seems to think he's been the victim of a dastardly crime spree. He's losing more inventory than usual from his candy stock."

"So you're fingerprinting the display rack? Forgive me, Chief Bowman, but that seems a little extreme, doesn't it?"

"I'm humoring Mr. Ashton," he admitted. "He's an elderly man and rather set in his ways. I tried to explain this was an exercise in futility since every single person in town has bought candy off this rack at some point. But he's got a bad heart and I didn't want to stress him more by arguing with him. Seemed easier to just lift a few prints."

She gazed at him for a long moment, as if he were a completely alien species she had just wandered across in the mountains.

Right now, he felt like one. "I know. It's stupid."

She shook her head, something warm and soft in her eyes. "I don't think it's stupid. I think it's...sweet."

He wasn't sure he really wanted her thinking he was sweet. He had been a police officer for the last decade and a military policeman for four years before that. He'd passed sweet a long, long time ago—if he'd ever been there at all. Before he could correct her misconception, he heard a high, childish voice shriek out his name.

"Trace! Trace! Trace!"

Both of them looked at the approaching cart, pushed by a woman with a swinging blond ponytail and a delighted smile that was only matched by the cherubic two-year-old with the inky black curls and the huge dark eyes who was waving madly at him from the front seat of the cart. "Hi, Trace. Hi, Trace!"

He smiled at Easton Springhill Del Norte and her adopted daughter, Isabella. "Hey, you. Two of my favorite people!"

Belle held her arms out for him to hug her in that generous, loving way she'd been blessed with despite her haphazard early years. "How's my girl?" he asked and was rewarded with an adorable giggle.

"I'm good. Mommy said I could have a juice box in the car if I'm good while we're shopping."

"That's a brave mommy. You'll have to be careful not to spill it."

"I won't. I'm a big girl."

"I know you are." He eased her back into the seat and kissed Easton on the cheek, strangely aware of Becca watching them. "Becca, this is my favorite two-and-a-half-year-old, Miss Isabella Del Norte, and her mother, Easton."

Becca gave a stiff sort of smile. "Hi. I think you've come into the diner a few times."

"Oh, right." Easton beamed. "You're the new waitress, Wally Taylor's granddaughter. It's great to formally meet you."

"How are you, East?"

"I'm great." She gestured to her baby bump, about the size of a bocce ball. He knew she was expecting in March. "Beginning to waddle. Another few weeks and I won't be able to get up on a horse, I'm afraid. Cisco's already making noises about me taking a break from calving this year."

"You look beautiful," he told her, completely the truth. She had always been lovely to him, but he couldn't deny that since Cisco Del Norte had stopped his wandering and settled down in Pine Gulch and they had married, Easton had bloomed.

Trace could admit now that he'd been worried the man would break her heart all over again and leave like he'd been doing since they were just kids, but by all appearances, Cisco seemed like a man who wasn't going anywhere, who loved his family and raising horses and living in a small Idaho town. He'd even helped Trace out a few months ago on a drug case with South American ties, Cisco's specialty after years as an undercover drug agent.

A few years ago, Trace had wanted much more than friendship with Easton. They had dated several times and he had been pretty sure they were moving toward something serious when Cisco had returned home. When he saw how much Easton loved the other man, Trace had stepped aside. What else could he have done? He couldn't regret it, not when their joy together was obvious to everyone around them, but once in a while when he saw her, he couldn't help the little pang in his heart for what might have been.

"I need to finish shopping and check out," Becca said. "I'll see you later."

"I'm sorry we interrupted your conversation," Easton said. "It's wonderful to meet you."

Becca gave a polite smile and headed around the next aisle. He watched her go for a moment. When he turned back, he found Easton studying him carefully.

"She seems very nice."

"How do you know? You barely exchanged two words with her."

She gave a shrug and tucked a stray blond lock behind her ear "I've got a vibe about these things. She's very pretty. I heard she has a daughter. Any husband in the picture?"

"East." He glared at her, which she parried with an innocent look.

"What? I was just asking."

"As far as I can tell, no. No husband in the picture."

"Good. That's very good. I'll have to make sure Jenna sends her an invite to the Cold Creek Christmas party at the McRavens' so I can get a chance to sit down with her for a real visit."

"You don't need to vet women for me, East," he growled. "I do fine on my own."

"Do you?" Though her voice was teasing, he didn't miss the concern in her eyes. "You know I love you and only want the best for you. You deserve to be happy, Trace."

He wasn't sure a woman like Becca Parsons, who obviously didn't trust him, was the route to happiness.

"I am happy. I've got a great life, full of interesting people and darling little shoplifters." He grabbed the pack of gum out of Belle's chubby little fingers that she must have lifted when neither he nor Easton were looking.

"Belle. No, no," Easton exclaimed.

"I like gum."

Trace laughed. "I'm sure you do, honey. But you'd better be careful or Ralph Ashton will throw you in the slammer."

This was about the only time she *really* missed Arizona.

Since she left for work, the snow had been falling steadily. At least four inches now covered the sidewalk and driveway that she had just shoveled first thing in the morning before she headed for the breakfast shift.

What she wouldn't do for a few saguaro cactuses in her line of vision right about now, the beige and browns and grays of living in the desert. Instead, she was surrounded by snow and icicles and that very cold wind that seemed to sneak through her parka to pinch at her with icy fingers.

For three days, Mother Nature had been relentlessly sending flurries their way.

It was the worst kind of snow, too—not a big whopping storm that could be taken care of in one fell swoop, but little dribs and drabs spread over several days that had to be shoveled a few inches at a time.

She was already tired of it and had been reminded several times by customers at The Gulch that winter was really only beginning. She did have to admit she was looking forward to what everyone told her were spectacular summer days—and wondrously cool nights. During the summer in Phoenix, it was often still ninety degrees at midnight.

"We tell people hereabouts, if they complain about the winter, they don't deserve the summer," Donna had told her a few days earlier.

She scooped another shovelful of snow, wishing her budget would stretch for a snowblower. As it was, she would be lucky to be able to give Gabi a few toys and books for Christmas. She was picking up a few things here and there for the girl. Money was tight but she was managing—and she was more excited about the holidays than she might have believed possible even a few weeks earlier.

Much to Becca's befuddlement, Gabi loved to shovel the snow. She ought to leave the driveway for another few hours until her sister came home from school, but Becca was afraid if she waited much longer, it would be so deep it would take hours to clear. As it was, by the time she finished the curve of sidewalk leading to the house, her biceps burned and her lower back was already beginning to ache.

She started on the driveway when she heard an approaching vehicle heading down the street. To her surprise, the vehicle slowed and then stopped in front of her house. Through the whirl of snow she recognized the white Pine Gulch Police Department SUV and she suddenly felt as warm as a Phoenix afternoon in July.

Trace climbed out of the SUV and headed toward her. He wore a brown shearling-lined police-issue parka and a Stetson and he looked rough and gorgeous. She, by contrast, felt frumpy and bedraggled in her knit hat and gloves and the old peacoat that wasn't quite as effective as it should be against the weather.

He smiled warmly and she suddenly felt breathless from more than just the exertion of shoveling.

She hadn't seen him since that day in the store, nearly a week earlier, though she had seen his vehicle pass by a few times when she'd been up late at night.

He looked tired, she thought, with a pang of sympathy for his hard work on behalf of the good people of Pine Gulch.

"Need a hand?" he asked.

She ought to tell him no. Every moment she spent with him only seemed to make her hungry for more. But the driveway was long, the snow heavy, and she was basically a weak woman.

"As long as it has a shovel attached to it, sure."

He opened the back of his SUV and pulled out a snow shovel, then dug in without a word.

They worked mostly in silence on different ends of the driveway, but she didn't find it uncomfortable. She wanted to ask him about the woman in the grocery store and what his feelings for her were. They were plainly friends but she gained the distinct impression in the store that the two of them had shared more than that. Did it bother him to see her with one child and another on the way? Was he still in love with her?

None of those questions were any of her business, she reminded herself, shoveling a little more briskly.

Trace was obviously much more proficient at this particular skill than she was—and much stronger—and what would have taken her at least an hour was done in less than half that.

"Thank you," she said when the last pile had been

pushed to the side of her driveway. "That was a huge help."

"I told you, people in Pine Gulch take care of each other."

She was beginning to believe it. Much to her surprise, Becca was beginning to enjoy living in Pine Gulch. What had started out as only a temporary resting place while she tried to figure out what to do next had become familiar. She liked the fact that when she went to that quaint little grocery store in town, Trace hadn't been the only person who had stopped to talk to her. She had been greeted by two different people she'd waited on at the diner, each of whom had stopped her to make a little friendly conversation and wish her Merry Christmas.

"Just out of curiosity, why do you have a shovel in your vehicle?"

He smiled at the question. "For digging out stranded cars or helping the citizens of Pine Gulch with their snow removal needs. Even the reluctant ones."

She flushed. "I let you help, didn't I? I'm grateful. Believe me, you saved me all kinds of work. For the most part, I guess I'm used to taking care of myself."

"Nothing wrong with that. You should fit right in here in eastern Idaho. We're known for our self-sufficient resilience."

"You were probably on your way somewhere, weren't you?"

"Just home for a few hours of downtime and to put the dog out before I head back at six for another shift. I'm shorthanded right now, if you haven't figured that out."

"Well, I appreciate you spending a little of your

downtime helping me shovel when you've got your own to do. Would you like me to go help you with your driveway?"

"No need. I pay a neighbor kid to come over with his dad's snowblower. It puts a little change in his pocket and keeps him out of trouble. Plus, it makes things a little more convenient for me. With my shifts being all over the place, I never know when I'll be available to shovel the snow. This way I don't have to worry about it. I can give you his name if you'd like."

She considered her meager budget and how much paying someone to clear her driveway would probably cost through a long eastern-Idaho winter. Cheaper than buying a snowblower herself, she supposed, but until she was able to finish the waiver requirements for transferring her bar membership—which included a hefty fee, unfortunately—she would have to make do.

"I'm okay. I like the exercise," she lied. He didn't appear to buy the excuse. To divert his attention, she said the first thing she could think of. "Would you like to come in for some cocoa? It's the least I can do to repay you for helping me."

She didn't really expect him to say yes. Why would he want to spend any more of his brief leisure time with her? To her surprise he kicked the rest of the snow off his shovel and propped it against his truck. "I'd like that. Thanks."

Now she'd done it. She couldn't rescind the invitation without sounding like an idiot. At the same time, she wasn't sure being alone with Trace on a snowy December afternoon was the greatest of ideas, not with this awareness that seemed to pop and hiss between them.

She would be polite, would make him some cocoa

and then send him on his way. She had absolutely no reason to be nervous.

Reasonable or not, nerves jumped inside her as she opened the door to her grandfather's house and led him inside.

He should be stretched out on his recliner taking a nap right about now. For the last three weeks, he'd been running on about five hours of sleep a night or less and he was beginning to feel the effects. He should have just helped her shovel and then headed home. Her invitation to come inside had taken him completely by surprise and he'd agreed before he'd really thought through the wisdom of it.

"The tree looks great," he said. She and Gabi had added a popcorn-and-cranberry garland and homemade ornaments. Paper-cut snowflakes hung in the windows and across the door frame and it appeared as if she had cut some of the greenery from the evergreens out in the yard and tucked them on the fireplace mantel and on the banister up the stairs, threaded with lights and a few glossy ornaments. More greenery and ribbons wound through the old chandelier above the dining room table.

In the few weeks since he had been here helping them put up the Christmas tree, Becca had created a warm, welcoming haven out of Wally Taylor's dark and gloomy house. The house no longer looked like a sad old bachelor's house, years past its prime. Somehow on a budget of obviously shoestring proportions, Becca had created a cozy space full of color and light—plump, bright pillows on the old sofa, new curtains, a colorful quilt over the recliner.

He hoped the efforts she had expended into creating

a comfortable nest for her and for and her daughter indicated Becca intended to stay in Pine Gulch, at least for a little while.

"You've been hard at work. The place looks great," he said, ignoring the little spurt of happiness lodged in his chest when he thought about her giving his town a chance.

She looked embarrassed at the compliment. "It's still a dark, crumbling old house with outdated linoleum and ugly carpet. I can't do anything about that right now until I save a little more. But I own it outright and nobody can take it away from me."

An interesting comment that made him even more curious about her background. He wondered again what had led her here and what sort of insecurity and instability she might have faced that made her cling so tightly to the house.

"Let me take your coat," she said. "Sit down here by the fire and warm up a little while I fix the cocoa."

"I'll let you take my coat but this isn't The Gulch. You don't have to serve me here. I can help with the cocoa."

"It's not The Gulch but it is my home and you're a guest here."

As she reached for his coat, her fingers brushed his and that subtle awareness simmered to life between them again. Had he ever noticed the curve of her cheekbone before, that particularly unique shade of her eyes?

She was so lovely, soft and restful, and he just wanted to stand here for a moment with the little fireplace crackling merrily and the snow still falling steadily outside and simply enjoy looking at her.

He grabbed her fingers in both of his hands around his coat. "Your hands are cold," he murmured.

She stared at him, her eyes suddenly wide. He could hear the ticking of a clock somewhere in the house and the shifting of the house and the sudden whoosh as the furnace clicked on. A low hunger thrummed between them, glittery and bright. He could step forward right now and pull her into his arms, capture that lusciously soft mouth with his. He might not learn all her secrets that way but it would be a start.

The fire suddenly crackled and Becca blinked and the moment was gone.

She cleared her throat and tugged her still-cold fingers away. "I'll, uh, hang up your coat and see about the cocoa."

She headed back through the house. He followed her into the kitchen, with its dark-wood paneling and old-fashioned appliances. She had tried to brighten this room up, too, with new white curtains, a set of brightly colored dish towels hanging on the stove and a watercolor print on the wall above the small crescent table, an Impressionist painting of a small cottage with an English garden blooming around it.

She stood at the stove, pouring milk into a saucepan.

"I thought when you said cocoa you were going to make it from the mix," he said.

"I like the old-fashioned way, with powdered cocoa and milk. It only takes a minute, though. Would you like a cookie? Gabi and I made them last night."

"I would, thank you. I'm afraid I'm weak when it comes to holiday goodies."

He picked one up and tasted shortbread and raspberries from the jam center. "These are delicious!"

"Thanks."

"Is it a family recipe?" he probed, hoping to get some insights into her background.

She shrugged. "Probably. Someone else's family, anyway. I found it online."

Okay, so much for that subtle line of questioning, he thought ruefully. But after a moment she added, somewhat reluctantly, "I don't remember my own mother ever making cookies."

"She wasn't the domestic sort, then?" he asked.

Her laugh was small with a hint of bitter undertone that made him sad. "That, Chief Bowman, is an understatement."

He would have liked to pursue it but she once again deflected his inquiries by turning the conversation back to him. "What about your family?" she asked as she measured vanilla. "Was your mother the cookie-baking type?"

"Sometimes, when the mood struck her. When she wasn't busy with her work."

"What did she do?"

"She was an artist. Oil on canvas."

"Really?" She narrowed her gaze. "Margaret Bowman. Was that your mother?"

He blinked, surprised. His mother had only just started becoming commercially successful when she was killed. "Yes. How did you know?"

"I saw one of her paintings of Cold Creek Canyon in springtime hanging in the library the other day. It was absolutely stunning. It gave me a little hope that maybe there's more to Pine Gulch than snow."

He had forgotten that he and his siblings had donated one of her paintings to the library in memory of their mother. "Mostly she did it for fun and passion. I think she loved collecting art as much as she enjoyed creating it."

Her polite smile encouraged him to add more. "When she was a young girl growing up in southern Utah outside Zion National Park, she and her mother became friends with Maynard Dixon, who had a home there," he said of the great Western artist. "Dixon was fond of my mother and encouraged her talent. He even gave her a small oil painting depicting the area. Later she and my father acquired three more Dixon paintings, as well as a couple of Georgia O'Keeffes and a small Bierstadt. They were the cornerstone of their collection."

"You must feel so fortunate to have such beautiful pieces to enjoy in your family."

The familiar anger and helplessness burned through him. "We don't. Not anymore. The Dixons and O'Keeffes and the Bierstadt were stolen ten years ago, along with the rest of their collection, the night my parents were murdered."

She paused from stirring the milk on the stove, her eyes shocked and sympathetic.

"I'm so sorry, Trace. You said they died. I thought... perhaps an accident."

"No accident. They were victims of a robbery and had the misfortune to have seen the bastards who broke in."

"How terrible."

Usually he hated talking about this, hated the pity and that hint of avid curiosity he would see in people's eyes when the topic came up. With Becca, her concern felt genuine and he found an odd sort of solace in it.

"I don't care about the artwork, you know? I never

did. The paintings were beautiful, but I would have ripped them off the wall myself and given them to any passing beggar on the street if it could have saved my parents."

"I'm sorry."

"It breaks my heart they never had the chance to even know Destry, to see where Ridge has taken the ranch, to watch Caidy grow into a beautiful young woman."

His voice trailed off and he flushed, embarrassed that he had revealed so much of himself to her, but she only continued watching him with that quiet compassion. "You said they died right before Christmas."

"Right. December twenty-third, ten years ago."

"How difficult for you and your family. That must have made it even harder, coming so close to Christmas."

He never talked about this part, but for reasons he couldn't explain he felt compelled to add the rest. "I was home on leave from the marines. I'd just finished my second deployment to the Middle East and had only three months left in my commitment to the military. I was trying to figure out what to do with my life, you know? Trying to figure out if I should re-up or get out. I spent most of my leave partying. Drinking. Staying out late. Living it up. Don't get me wrong, I loved my parents, my family, but I was a stupid kid. I met a girl and we were…"

His voice trailed off and he was angry all over again at his stupidity. He should have known something was wrong. He'd been a military policeman, for God's sake. But a devious little witch had thrown his natural instincts all to hell.

"I think I can figure out what you were doing," Becca said, a hint of dryness in her tone.

His jaw worked. "She was in on it. Her job was to keep me busy and away from the ranch while the rest of the crew went in and did the job. My parents weren't supposed to be home. My sister had a school choir concert. But at the last minute, she got sick and so they all stayed home. My dad surprised the thieves and he was shot first. My mom tried to run and they got her next. Caidy was hiding in the house the whole time. She still won't talk about it."

Her eyes drenched with sympathy, she poured cocoa into a mug with a snowman on it and then set it in front of him before taking the seat across the table from him.

"That's why you became a police officer? Your parents' murders?"

He looked into the murky depths of his drink where he could still see the swirl of cocoa from her spoon. "Yeah. Something like that. The age-old quest for truth, justice and all that idealistic garbage."

"I don't think it's garbage. Not at all! What's idealistic about wanting to protect the town and the way of life you love? It's honorable. You've tried to build on your parents' legacy, to keep Pine Gulch a safe place. At heart, you just want to make sure others don't have to cope with the same pain you and your brothers and sister have to live with. I get it."

He gazed at her for a long moment, then shook his head. "How do you do that?"

"What?"

"You're as good as any detective." He sipped at his cocoa, decadently rich. "You've definitely got a gift for getting people to reveal things they wouldn't normally talk about. I never intended to dredge up old history."

"I'm sorry if I was probing," she said, her movements and her tone suddenly stiff.

He had the oddest feeling he'd offended her somehow. What had he said? He combed through their conversation but didn't have the first idea what he'd done. "You weren't probing at all, Becca. That's not what I meant. I'm the one who mentioned my parents in the first place. I opened the door."

On impulse, he reached across the table for her fingers. Where they had been cold from shoveling snow before, her time in the kitchen and holding the mug of cocoa had left them warm, and he slid his thumb across the soft knuckle of her forefinger. "To be honest, if anything, I'm surprised at myself for telling you all the grisly details. It's a…touchy subject and I usually don't like to talk about it."

"Thank you for sharing it with me," she said solemnly.

Her fingers trembled a little in his. This close to her, he could see she had a little scar at the corner of her mouth and he wondered where it came from. He very much wanted to kiss her, even though he knew it probably wasn't very smart. He sensed once his mouth touched hers, he wouldn't want to stop. He would be perfectly happy to go on kissing her all afternoon while the snow fluttered down outside.

Any trace of fatigue seemed to have completely left his system. Instead, a fierce hunger settled low in his gut. With a long sigh, he finally surrendered to it, leaning across the table and brushing his mouth against hers.

She inhaled a sexy little breath at the first touch of

his mouth on her warm, soft lips and then she kissed him back. She tasted sweet and rich, intoxicating, with that earthy undertone of cocoa, and he wanted to sink into her and never bother climbing back out.

Chapter Six

This couldn't be happening.

She couldn't really be kissing the chief of police in the kitchen of her grandfather's house while the old refrigerator hummed and the wind blew snow under the eaves.

No, it was real enough. She seemed hyperaware of each of her senses. The noises of the house seemed magnified, each taste and smell more intense.

He tasted of cocoa and hot male and he smelled like laundry soap and starch and a very sexy aftershave with wood and musk notes.

As she had expected, Trace Bowman kissed like a man who knew exactly how to cherish a woman, who would make sure she always felt safe and cared for in his arms. He explored her mouth as if he wanted to taste every millimeter of it and wouldn't rest until he knew every single one of her secrets.

What started as just a casual sort of brush of his mouth against hers quickly seemed to ignite until she couldn't manage to string together any sort of coherent thought except *more*.

With their mouths still connected, he pulled her to her feet so that he could tug her closer and he leaned back against her counter, taking her with him. His heat and the strength of him seemed to enfold her and she wanted to stay right here with her arms wrapped around his waist and his mouth licking and tasting her until she could barely stand up.

She could feel his heartbeat—though perhaps that was hers, racing a mile a minute.

In her entire life, she had never gone from zero to *take-me-now* so quickly. She had known, somehow. From that first day, she had guessed that if she ever kissed Trace Bowman it would be an unforgettable experience, a kiss with the power to make her forget everything else except this.

She had no idea how long they kissed. It might have been days, for all she would have cared. They might have continued indefinitely, except the mantel clock suddenly chimed through the house, yanking her back to her senses.

She slid her mouth away, nearly shivering at the sudden chill. Calling on every skill at deception she had tried to suppress her entire adult life, she eased back and tried not to reveal that she wanted nothing more than to climb right back into his arms.

He stared at her, his breathing ragged and his eyes a hazy, hungry green. After a moment, he let out a breath. "Again. Not what I intended."

She had kissed men before. Heavens, she'd been

nearly engaged three months ago. But she had never been so completely rocked off her foundation by the touch of a man's mouth on hers.

Becca swallowed, reminding herself she was a mature woman who had graduated from law school, passed the Arizona state bar, been an associate at an extremely successful real-estate law firm in Phoenix. This was only a kiss. Nothing to leave her reeling and stunned.

The smart thing to do would be to get out in front of this before she blew the whole thing out of proportion.

"Was that a just-between-neighbors kiss or a let's-jump-into-bed-right-this-minute kiss?"

For an instant, he looked taken aback by her frankness and then he gave a rough-sounding laugh. "If we have to categorize it, why don't we say it was more a we've-got-something-between-us-so-why-don't-we-just-see-where-this-goes? sort of thing."

She was tempted. So tempted. Trace Bowman was the kind of man she had dreamed about since she was old enough to know the difference between real men and her mother's usual boy toys. Decent and kind, he loved his family, he seemed grounded, he worked hard. Not to mention the minor little fact that he was the most gorgeous man she'd ever met and made her forget her own name.

But she had a million reasons why let's-see-where-this-goes wasn't a possibility for her right now. In some ways, she almost would have preferred the let's-jump-into-bed scenario. Her mind was already there, imagining tangled limbs and hard muscles and toe-curling passion.

"Look, I appreciate your help with shoveling the snow and the Christmas tree and everything. You've been very kind to Gabi and me and I'm grateful. It's just…to be perfectly honest, I'm just trying to keep my head above water here. Our situation is…complicated. I'm not in a really good place right now for, um, seeing where things go with you right now."

She couldn't gauge his reaction to what she said. Something flashed in his expression but he concealed it quickly and she couldn't tell if it was hurt or disappointment or neither. Finally he nodded. "Fair enough. Maybe once you've had time to settle in a little more, you'll be more of a mind to stop and look around and enjoy the view."

"Maybe," she said in what she hoped was a noncommittal tone. For just a moment she allowed her mind to imagine how things could be with Trace. More incredible kisses like that. Someone to lean on. Warm feet cuddling with hers on cold December nights.

Heavenly. If circumstances were different, she would love nothing more. He seemed like the genuine thing, a decent and caring man who wouldn't walk away at the first sign of trouble. But how could she ever allow herself to be involved with a police officer now when she and Gabi were basically living a lie? Before she could ever be in a relationship with Trace, she would have to tell him the truth about her, about Gabi, about Monica— and if she did that, admitted her deception, she knew Trace would be furious and hurt and wouldn't *want* any more delicious let's-see-where-this-goes kisses.

The sound of the front door opening and then closing again distracted her from the ache of regret settling somewhere near her heart.

"Why is there a cop car outside?" Gabi called out from the entry. "Is everything okay? Becca?"

With an inward cringe, she shot a quick glance at Trace to see if he noticed her "daughter" calling her by her first name. His expression was shuttered and expressionless and, again, she couldn't gauge his reaction.

Becca quickly straightened her sweater and smoothed a hand over her hair to make sure it wasn't flying in every direction. "In here, honey," she called, forcing a smile.

A moment later, Gabi walked into the kitchen, still wearing her snow-dotted parka and backpack. "Oh," she exclaimed when she saw Trace, and to Becca's consternation something that looked suspiciously like guilt flashed in her little sister's eyes before she blinked it away.

Oh, Gabi. What are you up to?

Gabi took in the plate of cookies on the table, the two coffee mugs half-full of cocoa and both of them standing only a foot or so apart, and her eyes narrowed with wary confusion.

"Hi, Gabrielle." Trace's smile could have melted every icicle dripping from the roof. "You're home from school early, aren't you? School doesn't get out for another hour."

Gabi took off her beanie with a too-casual shrug that did nothing to alleviate Becca's worry. "I had a stomachache. I think I just need to lie down."

For about a second and a half, Becca was tempted to let her. The whole stomachache thing was an obvious lie but until she could get Trace out of the house, she couldn't call her sister on it. Whatever trouble she suddenly suspected Gabi might be tangled up in, this was something better handled outside the presence of an entirely too sexy police chief.

Aware of him watching their byplay with interest, she forced an expression of maternal concern. "Honey, you can't just leave school like that, especially with all the snow out there. You should have called me so I could come pick you up."

"I figured you'd be busy." Gabi's gaze shifted from Becca to Trace and back again, "Looks like I was right."

She flushed, grateful Gabi hadn't barged in five minutes earlier. "Did you tell your teacher or anyone else in the office you were leaving?"

Gabi didn't say anything and Becca's stomach twisted. The last thing they needed was trouble at school, any unusual behavior that might raise eyebrows and cause unwanted speculation. Gabi darn well knew they were trying to fly straight in Pine Gulch. Well, mostly straight.

"I didn't think about it," she said defensively. "We had a late-afternoon recess. I went in to go to the bathroom and decided to just grab my backpack and come home. I thought it would be okay. I mean, school was almost over, right? We're only a few blocks from the school anyway and I just thought it would be faster for me to walk home instead of calling you."

She needed to get Trace out of here so she could have a straight conversation with Gabi without the darn chief of police looking on. She let out a breath, hating this tension churning through her. Lies and deception. Her entire life from her earliest memories was a writhing, tangled mess of them and she hated it.

"I'll call the school and let them know you've come home so they don't worry about you. We wouldn't want them reporting you missing to the police or something."

She tried to make a joke of it but neither Trace nor Gabi even cracked a smile.

"Next time, you need to go through the proper channels, okay? I can come to the school to pick you up, no matter what I might be in the middle of doing." Like kissing the Pine Gulch police chief until she couldn't think straight.

"Okay. May I please go to my room to lie down?"

Definitely un-Gabi-like behavior. She frowned at her sister but didn't know how to probe while Trace was still there.

"Yes. It should be warm and toasty up there. I'll come check on you in a few minutes." She rubbed a hand over Gabi's hair, a little damp from the snowflakes that had seeped through her beanie.

"I'm sorry," Gabi muttered.

"No worries. I'll call the school. Go get some rest."

The girl escaped quickly and Becca pulled her cell phone from her pocket. She had added Pine Gulch Elementary to her address book when they first moved to town and she found it quickly and dialed.

"Hello," she said when the secretary answered. "This is Rebecca Parsons. I'm sorry for the mix-up, but my sis—" She caught herself just in time and didn't trust herself to look at Trace to see if he'd caught her mistake. "My *daughter,* Gabrielle, just came home with a stomachache. I'm afraid she walked here on her own without letting her teacher or anyone at the office know."

She listened to the secretary's stern admonitions about following procedures. "Yes, I've told her she shouldn't have left like that. We had a long talk about it and I don't believe she'll do it again. I just wanted you to know she is home and safe and will be out for the remainder of the day."

"Tell her to drink fluids and get plenty of rest," the secretary said. "There are some nasty bugs going around right now. We've had five children go home sick today."

"I'll do that. Thank you, Mrs. Gallegos."

She ended the call and turned back to Trace. "Apparently there's a mini-epidemic at Pine Gulch Elementary School."

"Should I be calling in the Center for Disease Control?" He asked the question with a smile that made her heartbeat skip, made her wish she could forget everything and just sink into his kiss once more.

"I don't believe so. Good to know it's an option, though."

"Since it looks as if you've got your hands full, I'll take off. Thank you for the cookies and cocoa and... everything."

Her mind replayed the heat of his mouth on hers, his body hard and solid, his arms wrapping her close...

"Thank you for helping me clear the driveway."

"You're welcome. I'm afraid you're only going to have to head out again in a few hours and do it all over again."

Through the kitchen window, she could see big, fluffy flakes slanting past and she sighed. "You know, if I were in Phoenix right now, I wouldn't have to worry about the snow."

Or the ache in her feet from standing all morning in the diner or keeping the power bill paid or how she was going to put food on the table for a growing nine-year-old girl after her mother cleared out her savings and her equity.

Or sexy, perceptive police chiefs that made her want to throw all her troubles to the wind and jump into his arms.

"I'm glad you're not in Phoenix," he said with a half smile, and despite all the stress and worry and snow, for this moment, she was, too.

After Trace donned his police-department coat and Stetson again and headed out the door, Becca returned to the kitchen and fixed a tray of saltines and some of the orange-pineapple juice Gabi liked, then headed up the stairs.

Though there were two other bedrooms besides her own on the main floor, Gabi had chosen a room up here, a small, cramped little space under the eaves with a sharply angled ceiling and dormers at both ends.

She knocked outside the door and after a long pause, Gabi finally said, "Come in."

With her first weekly paycheck from The Gulch, she and Gabi had driven to Idaho Falls where the shopping selection was a little better and purchased a can of pale lavender paint and a cheerful comforter set to make the space more homey.

Despite those feeble decorating efforts, Gabi hadn't done anything to put the stamp of her considerable personality in the room. Other than the warm, fluffy comforter and the fresh coat of paint over the tired old beige, the room seemed barren and lifeless.

Becca understood her sister's psyche entirely too well. Given her track record with Monica, Gabi didn't expect to be here long, so why bother trying to make the room feel more like home? Her heart ached for her sister, for all the rooms she had probably settled into, only to be yanked out again when Monica moved on to the inevitable greener pasture.

"How are you feeling?" she asked, setting the small tray on the narrow table beside the bed.

"Okay."

She reached out to feel Gabi's forehead and wasn't really surprised when the girl flinched away from the contact. Gabi didn't want to let Becca past her defenses any more than she wanted to settle into the house.

"You don't have a fever. Not that I'm an expert, you understand, but as far as I can tell you don't feel warm. Do you think you're going to be sick?"

"No. I'm okay now. It was probably just something I ate."

Her gaze shifted to the drawer of the bedside table then quickly away again, making Becca wonder if Gabi had perhaps stashed junk food in there and was eating it until she was sick. That was another hallmark of someone with an uncertain childhood—stockpiling food for those times when Monica was too busy with her latest scheme to remember minor little details like feeding her child.

One part of her wanted to let Gabi keep whatever security measures she needed to feel safe, but this was one of those situations where Becca knew she needed to be the adult, not hearken back to that scared child, tucking a jar of peanut butter and a spoon under her bed, just in case. She resolved to find a moment over the weekend to look through Gabi's room when she had a chance.

Not now, though, when Gabi said she had a stomachache.

"Can I get you anything?" Becca asked.

"No. I think I'll just try to finish the book I'm supposed to for my oral report next week and then maybe take a nap."

Though she detested her homework, there were moments when Gabi sometimes acted more like a particularly responsible college student than a nine-year-old. Becca still found them unnerving.

She couldn't shake the feeling that something else was going on with Gabi, that the girl was perhaps in some kind of trouble. She wasn't great at reading her sister but there was an air of suppressed excitement about Gabi underneath her mien of solemn illness. Becca's early years with Monica had left her rather good at sensing subtexts and layers. It had also taught her the futility of fighting a losing battle. Right now, Gabi seemed completely closed off to her.

"Does anything sound good to you for dinner?"

Gabi's shove rippled the comforter tucked under her chin. "I'm not hungry. Just fix whatever sounds good to you. If I'm feeling okay, I'll try to eat something later."

"Okay. Get some rest." She smoothed her sister's hair away from her face, wondering how it was possible for this curious little creature to become so dear to her in a few short, extremely stressful months. Oh, she might occasionally long for the life she'd had before Monica and Gabi had burst back into it, probably in the way any new parent might pine for their single, carefree life at random moments.

Protecting and caring for Gabi had become the most important thing in her world. She loved Gabi and would do anything necessary, even wait tables for ten hours a day, to make sure her sister never had to squirrel food away again.

She tucked the comforter a little more snugly around her sister, then turned toward the door. Gabi's voice stopped her before she reached it and she turned.

"I really am sorry I left school like that. I just... didn't want to be at school anymore. I mean, not if I was going to be sick or something. I didn't want to puke in front of the other kids. Will we be in trouble now?"

"I called and spoke with the school secretary. I promised her it wouldn't happen again. It won't, right?"

"No. It was a stupid mistake. I should have followed the rules better."

Gabi sounded so disgusted with herself, Becca was compelled to return to the bed and pull her sister into a hug.

Though Gabi tended to shy away from physical encounters like a kitten who'd had one to many encounters with a stern broom, this time she yielded in Becca's arms and she could swear she even felt her sister return the hug for a moment before she dropped her arms and eased away.

Progress. One little step was still forward momentum.

"Get some rest now. I'm sure Donna won't mind if I take tomorrow off and I'm not working Sunday so that will give you the weekend to recover."

"You don't have to take time off. I'm fine staying here by myself."

She wasn't going to let that happen anytime soon. "We'll see. Maybe I can see if Morgan Boyer can babysit you again."

"I don't know why you won't let me stay alone. Mom did it all the time."

She was *not* their mother. She had spent her entire adult life making sure of that. "We'll figure something out." She headed for the hallway. "I'll leave your door open. Call down the stairs if you need anything."

"I won't."

Of course not. Gabi thought she was this self-contained little adult who didn't need help from anyone. She left the door ajar but by the time she made it to the bottom of the stairs, she heard the click of Gabi closing it firmly behind her.

Becca sighed, fighting the urge to march back up the stairs and open the door again. Gabi was doing her best to keep her out. The only thing she could do was keep pouring love on her sister and she had to hope she would eventually reach through that prickly skin to the sweet girl she knew lived inside Gabi.

Chapter Seven

Sunday evening, Trace sat in the two-storied great room at River Bow enjoying the warmth of the fireplace and the flickering Christmas tree lights and the sight through the huge picture window of the last rays of the dying sun reflecting a pale orange on the snow.

He'd had a hell of a few days and was in dire need of a little quiet. The storm Friday and Saturday had snarled up the roads, resulting in numerous traffic accidents. And then that stupid jackass Carl Crenshaw had spent all day Saturday watching college football games and steadily drinking, trying to drown his sorrows at being laid off from the county road crew. When his wife tried to get him to turn the television off for dinner, he'd ripped down the mounted trophy six-point deer rack he'd shot the previous fall and gone after his wife with it, while their three kids watched.

Now Connie was in the hospital in Idaho Falls with

a broken arm and multiple stab wounds and Carl was in the county jail and their three little kids had probably been traumatized for life.

Trace needed a little peace and lighthearted chatter. Unfortunately, he wasn't finding much of it here. His twin brother could usually be counted on for a laugh but he was on duty. Ridge was busy with ranch paperwork, Caidy had kicked him out of the kitchen and Destry seemed subdued and distracted.

She sat silently beside him reading a book while he flipped through channels, not in the mood to watch football after the Crenshaw domestic dispute. Wally Taylor's ugly little dog sat at her feet, chewing on a rawhide bone Caidy had produced for him when they arrived.

Finally her silence became too much and he turned off the television. "Okay, spill. What's going on? Doesn't Christmas vacation start later this week? You should be hyped up on sugar and bouncing off the walls right about now."

She gave him an exasperated look. "I'm nine years old, Uncle Trace. I don't bounce off walls."

A few months ago on her birthday, she'd basically done exactly that, but he decided not to embarrass her by reminding her of it. "Okay, maybe you're too old for bouncing off walls but you should at least be in a good mood," he said. "It's Christmas! What are you asking Santa to bring you?"

"Nine years old, remember?" she pointed out. "I don't believe in fairy tales like Santa Claus and the Easter Bunny anymore."

"Now, that's just sad," he said. She was growing up, no longer the cute little bug who used to jump into his arms when he walked through the door. In a few short years she would be a teenager—ack!—and not have time for him anymore. Before that happened, he would have to make sure all the young men in town remembered her uncle was the chief of police.

"Okay, scratch Santa, then. What are you asking your dad to get you for Christmas?"

Caidy walked in at that moment carrying a bowl of her creamy, delicious mashed potatoes, which she set on the dining table. "Wrong question."

"Why's that?" he asked.

"We're having issues in that arena," Ridge answered, coming down the hall from the ranch office with a stack of paperwork in his hand.

"What's the matter?" Trace winked at Destry. "Are you asking for a new Ferrari again?"

She frowned. "No. It's not a big deal. I don't know why everybody's so mad."

"Nobody's mad, honey," Caidy said. "Just concerned about what's going on. You have to admit, it's unusual."

He thought things had been better with his niece. After he and Taft had talked about the problem a few weeks ago, she had seemed to cheer up and had become excited about Christmas again. Apparently he was out of the loop around the ranch. He'd missed dinner the week before thanks to his crazy December schedule and hadn't given Destry much thought.

"What's so unusual? What's going on?" he asked as they all converged on the table and took their usual places.

"It's not a big deal," Destry repeated. "I only asked for money this year instead of presents. You'd think I robbed a bank or something."

"Money for what?"

"There's the rub," Ridge muttered. "She doesn't want to tell us. She insists it's her business. I don't know how any kid can expect her parents to just hand over cash for Christmas or anything else without having the first idea what it's going to be used for."

"It's not like I'm going to buy drugs or something! I wouldn't do anything bad with it, I swear, Dad."

"Then you shouldn't have a problem telling me what you want to do with the money," Ridge countered as he grabbed a fresh roll out of the basket and set it on the edge of his plate. "How do I know you're not going to run off and buy a train ticket to Hollywood?"

"You know I wouldn't do that. Jeez, Dad."

"Then what?"

"I don't know. Stuff. Books and clothes. Songs on iTunes. I'm nine years old. Maybe I would just like some money to spend the way I want it."

She looked down at her plate when she spoke but Trace didn't miss the slight flush on her high cheekbones. She was a lousy liar and they all knew it. She could never look any of them in the eye when she told a whopper. Ridge glanced at Trace, a help-me-out-here sort of look in his eyes, as if his position as chief of police gave him automatic lie-detector status.

"You get an allowance, right?" he asked. "Maybe you can talk to your dad about a raise. Why do you need more than that?"

"I just do." She spoke with the stubbornness she had inherited from her father. And her uncles and aunt, for that matter. None of the Bowmans had a reputation for backing down from an argument.

"Well, if money is what you want, I think that's what you should get."

His pronouncement was met with a grateful look from Destry, but Caidy and Ridge just glared at him.

"No, it's not," Ridge said.

"Why not? Makes it easier on the rest of us. Then we don't have to waste our time shopping for things she doesn't want. Like, I don't know, those new pink-and-black Tony Lamas with the flowers on them that somebody mentioned a few months ago."

He thought he had her there. For a few seconds, her eyes softened with wistful yearning but then she blinked and her expression grew resolute once more.

"Thanks, Uncle Trace." She rose from the table and came around to his side and wrapped her arms around his neck for a quick hug before returning to her seat. "Will you tell Uncle Taft?"

He nodded. "I'll tell him. But you know Taft and how much he likes to shop for pink flowered boots."

She giggled. "Dad, do you want me to say grace?"

Though Ridge was still glowering at Trace, he nodded to his daughter. "Make sure you ask a special blessing for your uncles to be safe while they work."

"I always do," Destry said, which sent a lump rising in Trace's throat.

After the dinner of pot roast and potatoes and Caidy's moist, delicious rolls, he and Ridge were relegated to kitchen duty while Caidy and Destry worked on homework on the recently cleared dining room table.

"So what's really going on with the whole Christmas present thing?" he asked his older brother as he washed dishes.

"Damned if I know. She came home from school with this harebrained request earlier this week and refuses to talk about it. She just says she wants money instead of presents." He shrugged. "Doesn't matter. I bought her a new saddle clear back last summer and I've been hiding it in the barn. Caidy's done most of the rest of her Christmas shopping already on the internet. We're not sending everything back."

Ridge dried and put the gravy bowl that had been their mother's on the top shelf of the cupboard. "Maybe you can talk to her. See if she'll tell you what's going on and why she needs money more than pink cowboy boots."

Trace frowned. "Why me?"

"You're the trained investigator. If you can't get anything out of her, I don't know who can."

"This is a little different than weaseling a confession out of a hardened criminal."

"With all your experience, getting a nine-year-old girl to tell you her secrets should be a breeze, right?"

He wasn't having much luck convincing Becca Parsons to confide her worries in him. But unlike the beautiful but secretive waitress, Destry already loved and trusted him. She might be a little more willing to confide in him.

After they finished washing the dishes and returning them to the cupboards, Ridge returned to the ranch computer in his office and Trace sauntered out to the dining table, where Destry and Caidy were working on a math assignment while Grunt plopped at their feet.

"How's the homework coming?"

She scribbled one more equation, then set down her pencil and closed her math book with satisfaction. "Done. Finally."

"Good. I was thinking, I bet my favorite girl has been

lonely. You want to come out with me to give Genie an apple?"

He counted on Destry's love for all the horses on the ranch to help persuade her to walk with him out to the barn for a little heart-to-heart.

"Sure," she exclaimed, looking much happier than she'd been all evening. "Just let me grab my coat."

A few moments later, they walked outside and headed for the barn. Grunt waddled along behind them, accompanied by a couple of the border collies Caidy rescued and trained. The December night was still, the kind of winter night when the world seemed to be holding its breath, waiting for something magical.

He walked the familiar path between the house and the barn, remembering all those years of having to wake before the sunrise to take care of chores before school. Though he had decided when he was a kid that ranching wasn't for him, he was still grateful for the lessons he'd learned here and the memories.

This had been the perfect place to grow up. Hidden trails to explore, a creek to play in on hot summer afternoons, a barn made for jumping into the hay from the loft. Wintertime had been sledding down the hill behind the barn, racing Taft on snowmobiles across the pasture, midnight rides into the mountains under a cold, starry night.

They had all been extraordinarily happy here, until that fateful night a decade ago. He pushed away the grim note, instead forcing himself to breathe in the scent of pine and cattle and that distinctive scent of impending snow.

At the barn, he headed immediately for his favorite horse, the buckskin mare he had trained seven or eight years earlier. She whinnied with delight when she saw him, more so when he produced her favorite treat, an apple, from his pocket.

While she lipped the treat, he rubbed her neck and withers while Destry refilled water troughs from the hose in the barn then came to stand beside him.

"I need to get out here one evening and take her for a ride," he said.

"Can I come with you?"

He had the strangest idea of taking Becca and her daughter along with them. They would enjoy it, he thought. Would she agree to come? Maybe he would broach the idea after the holidays, when things settled down a little for him. She wanted only friendship between them but maybe if she spent a little more time with him, she might be persuaded to consider something more.

"Sure thing, munchkin. It's a date."

They moved next to *her* horse, the sturdy little paint pony she had named the rather unoriginal Patches when she was about five years old. She chattered to Trace about school, about her friends, about her homework, about a slumber party she would be attending over Christmas vacation. Finally he swung the conversation toward his reason for inviting her out to the barn.

"So just between the two of us, what's the real story about your Christmas presents? Why do you want money instead of girl stuff this year?"

She was quiet for a moment but he could see in her eyes that she was bursting to talk about it. "You promise you won't tell my dad or Aunt Caidy?"

"Why would I want to tell them?" he said, careful not to make any vows he wasn't prepared to keep. People seemed to think they could lie to children with impunity but he'd never subscribed to that belief.

She seemed to take his evasion as proof he would stay mum. She looked around the barn one more time, as if fearing invisible eavesdroppers. Or maybe she was worried Grunt would tell tales. Then she turned back to him.

"I want to give it to my friend."

"Your friend?"

Destry nodded. "She's really sick. Maybe dying. Her mom…they can't afford the surgery she needs to get better. I don't want her to die. She's only nine. My age. Me and my friends decided to help her. Maybe we can even raise enough money so she can have the surgery."

Okay, he hadn't been expecting that. He tried to keep his finger pretty firmly on the pulse of Pine Gulch and he hadn't heard anything about a sick child who needed surgery. "What's wrong with her?"

"I don't know for sure what it's called but she has some kind of problem with her heart. It makes her tired and sometimes she can't even play at recess. She just has to sit on the swings. Don't you think that's sad?"

"Very sad," he agreed. "What friend is this?"

She looked away from him, her eyes on her horse. "I promised I wouldn't tell. She doesn't like people to know she's sick, so she only told about five of us in the class. Nobody else knows."

He frowned. "Really? Not even Ms. Hartford?"

"I don't think so. She said people treat her differently when they find out and she just wants to be normal."

That sounded feasible, if a little odd. "You can tell me, Des. I can keep a secret. It's part of my job sometimes. Maybe I can help you persuade your dad to forget about the Christmas presents this year if you let me in on it."

She chewed her lip, mulling it over. Patches nickered and Destry finally shook her head. "I can't, Uncle Trace. I promised."

"Does she act sick?"

"Just tired a lot. Friday she was so tired she couldn't stay awake in class. She ended up going home at afternoon recess."

He stared at her, picturing Gabi Parsons coming into the kitchen of Becca's house with her parka covered in snow. Had she looked like someone with a heart condition? She had seemed subdued and a little pale except for the spots of cold-weather color on her cheeks.

Gabi had a heart condition? She was sick, possibly dying? Oh, *damn.*

He thought of how solemn she seemed all the time and the significant looks that sometimes passed between Becca and her daughter. It was definitely possible. That could explain everything—the worry in Becca's eyes when she looked at the girl, her desperate efforts to provide for her child, that sense of fear, almost despair, he picked up sometimes.

He had picked up plenty of clues over the weeks that she had tumbled into tough times. Medical costs could certainly explain that. Maybe she had come to Pine Gulch to live in her grandfather's house so she could save money on rent in order to afford an expensive operation her child needed.

A tiny jagged pain lodged in his chest at the thought of Becca coping with this kind of fear on her own, of poor Gabi facing tests and hospitalizations and the thought that she might not survive.

No wonder she had pushed him away after that stunning kiss. The last thing she probably had any energy for or interest in was a new relationship, despite the attraction that simmered between them. He wished, more than anything, that she had trusted him enough to confide a few of her troubles to him. He couldn't have eased her burden, but sometimes the sharing of it offered its own comfort.

"You're not going to tell, right?" Destry asked anxiously. "You promised. Not my dad, not Aunt Caidy, not anybody."

He forced a smile for his niece through the ache in his heart. "What would I tell? I don't know a single thing except that Genie still likes apples."

She smiled back, nudging his shoulder with her head much the way his horse did when she was happy with him. What a great kid, he thought. At an age when most kids were completely egocentric, thinking the entire world should bow to their demands, Des was willing to give up all her Christmas presents to help her friend.

Becca should know how much Gabi's friends cared about her. Perhaps that would help lift her spirits.

Chapter Eight

She was *not* a crafty person. So what was she doing the week before Christmas with knitting needles and a skein of yarn, trying to fumble her way through making a scarf and hat set for Gabi?

This was completely stupid, an exercise in frustration. She was trying only because Donna Archuleta loved to knit and always brought a bag with needles and yarn and her latest project to work on during her rare downtime at the diner. Becca had made the mistake of asking her about it one morning and the next thing she knew, Donna had brought her a spare pair of needles and yarn and had taught her a few basic stitches.

With the zeal of a true devotee, Donna had insisted this would help Becca deal with the stress of moving and the holidays and starting a new job. Those were the stresses Donna knew about. For obvious reasons, Becca hadn't told Donna about the strain of working to fill the requirements for reciprocal bar admission to practice law in Idaho or the inherent difficulties of trying to be a parental figure to a girl she hadn't known a few months ago.

She dropped a stitch, her fourth in about an hour. Donna made it seem so effortless but Becca mostly found it a pain in the neck. She was determined to finish it, though, mostly to prove she could.

After fifteen more minutes, she dropped another stitch. Rats. She dug out the crochet hook and tried fixing it with the technique Donna had explained, but it was frustrating business.

Though it was just past nine, she knew she ought to be in bed. She had enjoyed the day off but had to be at The Gulch at six-thirty for the breakfast shift, another day of standing on her achy feet and pouring coffee. A few more moments, she told herself.

Christmas was only a week away and she regretted she didn't have more presents for Gabi, or the endless budget to buy them. A homemade matching scarf and beanie set was pretty tame as far as gifts went, but maybe it would help cheer Gabi out of her moodiness. The yarn had been free from Donna, so all she needed to spend on this was her time and aggravation.

She frowned up the stairs. Her sister had gone to bed an hour earlier, claiming exhaustion. Becca wasn't buying it. Something was definitely going on with the girl. She hadn't exhibited any signs of sickness or laid claim to any further stomachaches, but all weekend she had been acting strangely. Giddy one moment—as if she knew a secret no one else did—then morose and defeated the next. She seemed to have lost her appetite, too, and hadn't even seemed to enjoy making more cookies.

Becca had done her best to finesse the truth out of her sister but apparently her persuasive skills were on the rusty side. Gabi insisted everything was fine, that school was going well, that she was coming to enjoy her new friends. Her efforts to dig deeper than that with her sister earned her nothing. Apparently she was as lousy at parenting as she was at knitting. She sighed again. Okay, she wasn't *that* bad at knitting. She held up the scarf under the light. The crochet-hook trick had helped, though the yarn pulled a little more tightly in that area. Just like taking care of Gabi, she was doing her best. The job might not be perfect but she was trying, right?

She picked up the needles again and had finished another row when she heard a quiet rapping on the door. The hands on the carved mantel clock showed 9:20 p.m. Who on earth would be dropping in this late? Though this was Pine Gulch and not one of the bad neighborhoods in Phoenix, she was still wary. She was a single woman, alone here with her "daughter," and everyone who came into The Gulch probably knew it.

She set the knitting on the table beside her chair and moved to the door cautiously, wishing she had an extra set of needles so she could wield one as a weapon. Since she had only the one—the crochet hook had that unfortunate, well, hook that didn't seem particularly deadly—she picked up an umbrella from the stand behind the door. She wasn't going to let anybody hurt Gabi on her watch.

After a careful peek through the curtain on the old-fashioned door, she dropped the umbrella back in the stand, though her nerves weren't eased in the slightest to find the police chief standing on her doorstep.

As she reached for the doorknob, she had one of those random flashbacks of sneaking out the back door of a rented dive somewhere in Arkansas and slipping away through an alley while the police hammered on the front.

She wasn't doing anything wrong here, she reminded herself. Trace was a friend, of sorts—the closest thing, anyway, she had to a friend here in Pine Gulch besides Donna Archuleta.

She opened the door and shivered at the blast of cold air. It was snowing again, drat it. That was the first thing she noticed. Then she picked up the tension in his shoulders, the tight set to his mouth. He was obviously upset about something.

"May I come in?" he asked after she greeted him.

All her self-protective instincts urged her to make some polite excuse and slam the door. *It's not a good time. I just started a bath. I have to stir a pot of gravy on the stove. I'm in the middle of brain surgery.* Anything to keep at bay these dangerous feelings she was beginning to have for this dangerous man.

She remembered their kiss of a few days earlier, the heat of his mouth, the wild jumble of sensations twisting her insides. All weekend, she had tried to put those moments out of her mind but the memory of being in his arms would flash into her head at the oddest moments, like song lyrics she couldn't shake.

She was many things but she wasn't a coward. "Of course." She opened the door wide enough for him to step into the warmth of her living room. Little snow crystals had settled in his dark hair and they gleamed under her entry light.

"Sorry to barge in like this. You were probably in the middle of something."

"Not really. Nothing productive, anyway. I was trying to knit a scarf for Gabi."

"That sounds productive."

"Not when you're as lousy at it as I am. I'm glad for the break." That much was true, anyway.

"Please, come in. Can I get you something?"

"No. I'm fine. Thank you." He gazed at her for a moment, then shook his head. "Scratch that. I'm not fine. I'm in a dilemma and I'm not sure how to deal with it."

And he was coming to *her* for advice? She wasn't quite sure how to respond.

"I need to talk to you about something, but I gave my word to a C.I.—confidential informant—that I wouldn't reveal this information," he went on. "I keep my word, Becca."

"I'm sure you do," she answered. Everything she had come to know about Trace indicated he was a man of honor who would protect anyone who placed her trust in him.

Much to her surprise and further confusion, he reached out and gripped her fingers in his, cool from the night air. "On the other hand, I wouldn't be betraying any confidences or revealing any new information to *you,* obviously. How could I be, when you know all this already, right?"

Did she? Because right now all she knew was confusion and concern and the insane urge to stand here all night simply holding his hand.

"I'm just going to come right out and say it. I'm so sorry for everything. Why didn't you tell me?"

A tiny flicker of unease stirred in her stomach. "I'm afraid you're going to have to be more specific. Why didn't I tell you *what?*"

"Everything. About Gabi."

That unease grew to genuine foreboding. Somehow he must have discovered Gabi wasn't her daughter but her sister and that she had no formal guardianship of her. How? Had Gabi told someone at school, perhaps his niece? Did everyone in town know? Was he there to take Gabi away?

Wait. Don't panic. Not yet. To her surprise, he didn't seem condemning about her lies, merely sympathetic. She never would have expected such sanguinity from him.

She drew in a breath and slid her hand away from his and tucked it in the front pocket of her hoodie. "How did you…um…find out about Gabi?"

He smiled but it seemed oddly sad around the edges. "I can't tell you that. My C.I., remember? Look, you don't have to talk about it if you don't want to. Obviously you're a very private person and I understand and can respect that. But if you need anything, even just a shoulder, I'm here. How long have you been dealing with this on your own?"

It felt like forever. She thought of those terrible early weeks after Monica ran off when Gabi had been lost and frightened, grimly determined her mother was going to show up again any minute now. Becca had been furious with her mother, of course, for abandoning her child that way without a word…and then she realized

Monica had forged her name on several checks and withdrew nearly all her savings.

This was all before the forged mortgage paperwork had begun to show up and she realized how deeply her mother had entrenched Becca in her latest deception. It was the latest betrayal in a lifetime of them. Becca was a real-estate attorney. Monica had to know that even the slightest whiff of mortgage fraud could lead to disbarment.

Fortunately, the senior partners at her firm had trusted her when she explained the situation. They had helped her clean up the mess, though it had taken the rest of her savings and all her equity in her town house, all while she was also dealing with a damaged nine-year-old girl who didn't want to be with her.

Tears burned behind her eyelids. She was so very tired of carrying the weight of this by herself. She longed to share even a tiny portion of the burden with someone else for a few moments.

"About four months," she finally admitted.

"But this can be fixed, right?" His eyes were dark with sympathy and something else, almost like sorrow. She frowned. Something was wrong here. His reaction seemed far disproportionate to the situation.

"I don't see how," she said warily. "If you have any ideas, I'd love to hear them."

"Well, won't the surgery help?"

She stared at him, confused all over again. That unease bloomed again in her stomach. "I'm sorry. Back up the truck here. What surgery are you talking about?"

"Gabrielle's surgery. For her heart condition."

She blinked, feeling as if she'd stepped off a ledge

somewhere into an alternate universe. "Gabi has a heart condition?"

The sorrow in his eyes seemed to cloud over, like fog tendrils snaking through trees, giving way to a confusion that matched her own. Silence stretched between them and he finally sat down heavily on her grandfather's sagging old sofa. "Doesn't she?"

"No. Why on earth would you think so?"

His features seemed to harden. "Oh, I don't know. Maybe because my niece is asking for money in lieu of presents for Christmas this year so she can give the money to Gabi so you can afford her heart surgery."

That unease now exploded into full-blown panic and her stomach roiled. *Gabi, what have you done?*

"I'm sure there's some misunderstanding." *Please, God, let there be some misunderstanding.* "Gabi doesn't have a heart condition, I promise. She's perfectly healthy."

If anything, he looked even harder, like chiseled stone. "Explain to me, then, why my niece is asking for money this year instead of Christmas presents to pay for an unnecessary surgery for your daughter?"

Because Gabi had been fed a steady diet of schemes and cons by their mother and the sweet taste of the grift flowed through her veins. She didn't know whether to be more sad for her sister or for her victims.

"I can't answer that," she said grimly. "But I promise you, I'll find out."

"According to Destry, there are five other girls at Pine Gulch Elementary who also want to give up their Christmas this year to help your daughter."

Nausea churned through her. They were going to be in so much trouble. *Oh, Gabi. How could you do this?*

She closed her eyes for a moment, trying to figure out how to wade through these treacherous waters. Her face flamed and she was very much afraid she was going to be sick. She was exhausted suddenly. How many times had she been in this position, forced to make excuses— mostly to herself—for the people in her life? She had thought she was being so healthy and strong after cutting ties with her mother when she was barely sixteen. Those years had been terribly difficult, but the peace and serenity, the hard-fought security, had been worth the sacrifices.

Now here she was again in the same situation, and this time couldn't just walk away from her sister. Gabi didn't have anyone else.

"Gabi can be…overdramatic. She is also prone to, um, exaggeration. She might have started a story and gotten carried away."

His gaze narrowed. "Destry said she's dying."

Darn you, Gabi. They had to live in Pine Gulch. Her sister had to go to school now with these little girls she'd tried to con. Becca had to work at the café, where she was bound to encounter the little marks' angry parents.

Monica should have taught her one of the most basic rules of grifting: only an ill bird fouls its own nest.

"She's not dying, I promise," she assured Trace. Though by the time Becca was through with her, she might wish otherwise.

"I guess I'm going to have to take your word for it. I have to tell you, this whole thing seems really strange to me. I just can't see your average nine-year-old girl making up a story like this on her own."

And just like that, suspicion now swung back to her. *She* must have put Gabi up to it. What other explanation could there be? They were both in on it, planning to collect their ill-gotten gains by playing on the sympathetic instincts of gullible locals and then ditch Pine Gulch. It was a likely scenario, one she might have come up with herself.

She should have expected it, since the same thing had been happening her entire life.

Despite her frustration with her sister for shoving Becca into the firing line, thrusting her into this miserable position once more, she was aware of a vague feeling of hurt. Trace had kissed her. He had seemed determined to forge a friendship with her despite all her back-off signals and had urged her to give this attraction between them a chance. Yet he was very quick to jump to conclusions at the first sign of trouble.

It was irrational, she knew. The man *shouldn't* trust her. She had been lying about Gabi and her relationship to the girl since the moment she and Trace met. She had absolutely no right to feel hurt.

"Gabi is not your average nine-year-old," she said as calmly as she could muster.

"Has she made up a story like this before?"

Hundreds of times. She sighed. Gabi probably had been telling lies since she could talk. The girl deserved a normal life, but Becca didn't have the first idea how to convince her she wouldn't find one unless she shed all the bad habits of her first nine years.

"She has a vivid imagination." She picked her words carefully. "Sometimes it can get her into trouble. I'm sorry, Trace. I'll talk to her. I'll make sure she clears this whole thing up tomorrow at school, I promise."

"Destry has been really upset about this. I think this is the reason she has been acting so strangely the last few weeks, not eating and not showing much interest in her usual activities. She's a compassionate little girl and thinking Gabi was dying has shaken her up. I wouldn't be surprised if it's the same with the other girls.

"It was cruel of Gabi to play on their sympathies. Cruel and wrong. I absolutely agree. I will make sure she comes clean, I promise."

"Is she sleeping now?"

"Yes. And to be honest with you, I should be, too. I have to work an early shift in the morning." She rose, hoping he would take the hint. Coping with all the complicated layers of her attraction to him was beyond her capabilities right now when she needed to deal with this latest stress that no amount of knitting in the world could ever ease.

To her relief he stood, as well.

"She's really not dying." He said the words as both a statement and a question and Becca shook her head.

"She's fine, Trace."

"I'm glad for that, at least. It ripped my guts out to think of you having to cope with that kind of pain and worry by yourself."

She had plenty of pain and worry, just not that particular pain and worry. This was a very good reminder that life could always seem worse. At least she and Gabi were both healthy.

"Thank you for coming to tell me, Trace." She opened the door for him. "I'll deal with Gabi, you can be sure."

He looked as if he wanted to say something more but he finally nodded. "Good night, then," he said and walked out into the cold night air.

After she closed the door behind him, Becca leaned

against it, her emotions in turmoil. This was *her* fault. She had sensed something was up with Gabi even before her sister came home from school pretending to be sick the previous Friday. Instead of confronting it head-on and worming the truth from her sister, she had opted to ignore her instincts, ignore the whole situation. Because she had chosen the path of least resistance, Gabi's lies had now tangled them both up into a mess she didn't know how to escape.

Beneath her guilt with herself and her frustration with her sister and renewed worry about how they would be able to make a life here in Pine Gulch once Gabi's latest deception became common knowledge, Becca was aware of an aching sadness for what she had lost.

She might have told herself she couldn't allow a relationship with Trace, but some part of her still yearned. This was a firm reminder that they could never be more than casual friends. He was a sworn officer of the law and she came from a long line of felons and thieves. The smartest thing to do now would be to cling tightly to whatever hard-fought distance she could find, no matter how much it hurt.

Chapter Nine

Though she had been tempted to wake Gabi as soon as Trace drove away through the December night, Becca forced herself to wait until the morning. Their confrontation would come soon enough. Better to wait until she had a cooler head and a calmer heart.

Instead, she endured a mostly sleepless night, worrying about her sister and about how she was going to teach right and wrong—moral choice and accountability—to a girl who had spent nine years watching her mother take what she wanted regardless of the consequences to anyone around her.

She grabbed only a few hours of sleep and woke gritty-eyed, with an aching sadness trickling through her.

Used to fending for herself from all those years with Monica, Gabi always woke to her own alarm clock. She was dressed and sitting at the small table in the dingy kitchen with her cereal bowl when Becca finished showering and pulling her hair into her customary ponytail.

"Morning." Gabi smiled at her, much more at ease than she'd seemed all weekend. The irony didn't escape Becca. She reminded herself that somewhere inside Gabi was as sweetly innocent as any other nine-year-old girl, she just needed more help and guidance now than most, as difficult as it might seem.

She drew in a deep breath. Now that the moment had come, she didn't know where to start. Better to just plunge right in, she decided, like that first moment of walking outside into the frigid air.

"I had a late-night visit from the police chief last night. Gabi, we need to talk."

Gabi froze, the spoon still in her mouth. Alarm flickered in her eyes but it was quickly concealed. She pulled the spoon out and returned it to the bowl before she spoke.

"Those girls gave me that stuff. I didn't do anything. I was going to give it back today, I swear."

She closed her eyes, her worst fears confirmed. The girls in her class thought she was dying of a heart condition and Gabi was certainly smart enough to work the situation to her advantage.

"What stuff?"

Gabi pressed her lips together as if she wanted to call her words back. After a long pause, she reached into her backpack and withdrew a handful of items, then spread them on the breakfast table. An iPod Touch, a handheld game system, a slim silver cell phone. What fourth-grader had a cell phone? Becca wondered. Probably most of them.

"You told them you're sick, didn't you? That you have

a bad heart. That's why the girls in your class gave you those things."

To her credit, Gabi looked genuinely upset. Her face crumpled and a tear leaked from one eye. Either she truly regretted her actions or Monica had a serious contender for the most deceptive Parsons female. "I didn't mean for…for all this to happen, Becca. I swear, I didn't mean it."

"Why would you lie about something so terrible?"

"At first it was just a joke, you know?"

"No. I don't understand this at all. Explain how you could joke about having a serious heart condition."

"I didn't want to go to P.E. one day. We were doing that stupid crab soccer that I hate and I can't do. So I told one of the girls I had a heart problem and she helped me get out of class."

"Why didn't you just say you hated crab soccer?"

"I don't know. It was stupid. I felt bad about it right after and was going to tell her the truth, but…" Her voice trailed off and she looked truly miserable.

"What?"

"They were all so nice to me afterward, you know? Writing me notes, bringing me lunch, watching out for me on the playground." She looked down at the table. "I didn't want to be here and thought school was stupid. But after I lied about being sick, I felt, I don't know, *important,* I guess. They were even talking about having a benefit for me. I thought it was cool."

"And then the girls started giving you iPods and cell phones and talking about going without Christmas presents so they could give you the money instead?" She used her hard, sharp attorney's voice and Gabi looked up, startled and guilty.

"I didn't ask for any of that stuff, I swear! They all just gave it to me. I think they thought it would make me feel better or something. I was going to give it back and tell them you wouldn't let me keep it."

"But you weren't going to tell them you were lying."

Her sister's silence was answer enough and her frustration overwhelmed her. "For heaven's sake, Gabi. Pine Gulch is our *home* now. We're not going anywhere. Haven't you figured that out? These are neighbors and friends, not marks who are so stupid they deserve to be conned. People you can grift and then never see again. I can't believe Monica never explained the difference of that to you. What are those girls going to think now when they find out it's not true, that you don't have a heart condition and you're not dying?"

She could see by the shock on Gabi's features that the thought had never occurred to her. And why would it? She and Monica had never lived more than a few months at a time anywhere, always moving on to the next city, the next job. Her poor sister had never had a normal life. As far as Becca knew, she'd probably never had a real friend who lasted more than a few weeks. Of course she wouldn't have her focus on the long-term implications.

Her sister's words confirmed the assumption. "They won't want to be my friends now, will they?"

Oh, darn. She wanted to step in and fix this for her sister but she knew this was one of those problems Gabi simply had to deal with on her own. How could Becca undo a lifetime of her mother's example and help Gabi see she could find a better way of life than using other people for her own advantage?

The only thing that gave her hope was the knowledge

that she had grown up under the exact same circumstances and somehow came out the other side with this sometimes inconvenient moral compass she couldn't shake.

"It's going to take some work. Put yourself in their position. You lied to them. They won't like thinking you made a fool of them. Now you're going to have to be honest—tell them what you told me, about wanting them to like you. Believe it or not, honesty can take you a lot further than lies and deception."

Judging by her skeptical expression, Gabi didn't look as if she were buying that particular concept. Becca couldn't really blame her.

Gabrielle was quiet all the way to the diner. She tried rather halfheartedly to convince Becca she didn't feel well, still feeling sick from Friday, and thought she should stay home one more day.

Becca only raised her eyebrow and stared down her sister, and after a moment Gabi mumbled something about how she would probably feel better once she was at school. When they arrived, she slid into her favorite booth looking out over Main Street and propped her book open in front of her.

As Becca waited on customers, she tried to keep a careful eye on her sister. She was fairly positive she didn't see Gabi turn the page one single time. Still, Gabi barely looked up even when Becca set a hot chocolate topped with fluffy whipped cream in front of her.

A little remorse could go a long way, she reminded herself as she waited on The Gulch regulars. Gabi needed to suffer a little for what she'd done to deceive her friends. Pain was a harsh but effective teacher.

The regulars had been joined by one of their occasional members, the mayor of Pine Gulch, Quinn Montgomery, a distinguished-looking man in his sixties with a teasing glint in his eyes.

She passed out their orders, ending with the mayor. "Here you go, sir. Egg-white omelet with extra green peppers, just the way you like."

"Thank you, my dear." He gave her a warm smile. "I don't know how you keep straight what everyone prefers."

She returned his smile as she refilled coffee at the table. "My steel-trap mind, Mayor. It serves me well."

He laughed out loud at that. "Where can I get one of those? My Marjorie is always telling me I'd forget my head if it wasn't screwed on."

Becca smiled and moved on to the next table, feeling slightly better than she had since she woke up.

She might trip over her feet and struggle to pour a simple cup of coffee without spilling it all over the customer and herself, but Becca had been given the gift of a keen memory. She never would have survived law school that first terrible year without it.

She sometimes suspected her excellent memory for customer names and preferences might be the only reason Lou and Donna hadn't fired her after the first week for gross incompetence. She was not cut out to be a waitress, though she wanted to believe she was no longer a complete disaster.

A couple of construction workers next to the regulars' booth were just giving her their orders when the door to the diner opened and the chief of police walked in wearing khakis and his Pine Gulch P.D. parka, looking dark and masculine. Her heartbeat skittered and she shifted her body so she was turned away from the door, reluctant to face him after the awkwardness of the night before.

"Did you catch that?"

She looked down at the construction worker with a bushy beard that had taken over his face. So much for her memory. With Trace Bowman around, she forgot completely where she was and what she was doing. "I'm sorry. Can you repeat that?"

With a frustrated sigh, he gave her his order again, making sure she wrote it down dutifully this time. When she finished, she turned to head toward the kitchen to place the order with Lou and discovered Trace had stopped to talk to the mayor and the other regulars, which meant she had no choice but to walk right past him.

She might have expected him to gaze at her with wariness or even disdain after basically finding out her sister was running a con on the whole elementary school. Instead, he greeted her with a smile that felt very much like a warm kiss on the cheek.

"Thanks for meeting me here," she heard the mayor say as she moved past. "We've got to figure out what we can do about that pesky intersection once and for all. Three fender-benders there in two weeks are three too many. Becca, you mind if we take an empty booth?"

She turned back. "Um, no. Of course not. Take whichever table you'd like."

"Can you give me a minute first, Mayor?" Trace asked. "I see someone I need to have a word with."

"No problem. Do what you need to do."

Becca expected Trace to go talk to one of the other patrons. Instead, he headed toward the booth in the corner where Gabi sat pretending to read, the whipped cream now dissolved into her untouched hot chocolate.

Oh, she wished she had a customer nearby who needed something. She was consumed with curiosity and no small amount of dread. Would he lecture Gabi, chide her for lying? She wouldn't be able to hear them over the noise of clinking glasses and the hum of conversation in the diner.

She could *see* Gabi's reaction, however. Her sister's expression as she saw the chief of police headed toward her was painful to see, a mix of fear and embarrassment. Trace said something to her, and to her shock Becca watched a small smile blossom on her sister's features, the first one she'd seen all morning.

They talked for a moment longer and then Gabi actually laughed. Becca couldn't hear the sound of it from her position but she could see her sister's genuine smile, the way her eyes lit up as some of the fine-wrought tension seeped out of her.

In that instant as she gazed at the two of them, something hard and tight seemed to dislodge around her heart and crumble to pieces. The noises of the diner seemed to fade and she couldn't breathe suddenly as the shocking realization thundered through her.

She was falling for Trace Bowman, this man who took time out of his hectic schedule and left the mayor himself waiting so that he could cajole a smile and a laugh from a frightened young girl.

Oh, she was an idiot. He was a police officer. The *chief* of police, for heaven's sake. If he knew who she was, what she came from, he would want nothing to do with her. How could she have been so very foolish? She should have taken better care to keep him at a distance.

From the moment she had met him here at The Gulch, she should have done everything she could to discourage his attempts at friendship.

She knew what was at stake here. As she had told her sister just that morning, Pine Gulch was their home now. They had nowhere else to go. She was trying to be admitted into the bar, to open her own law practice.

Only an ill bird fouls its own nest. Her nest was well and truly fouled. Disastrously messed up. How would she be able to live here, make a life with Gabi, when she was foolishly falling in love with the chief of police?

"Hey, Becca, you mind topping me off?" Jesse Redbear gave her his toothless smile. The sounds of the diner filtered back through her head and she realized she was standing stupidly in the middle of the floor gazing into space with the pot of regular in her hand.

She forced herself to move forward. Out of somewhere deep inside, she manufactured a smile. "Here you go. Sorry about that."

"Everything okay, hon? You look kind of pale." Sal Martinez gave her a worried look.

"I'm fine. Just fine." She shoved this latest disaster into the compartment in her head labeled "later" and pasted on what she hoped was a charming smile. "I can't believe it's snowing again. Doesn't it ever stop around here?"

"Sure," Jess said with his wheezy two-pack-a-day laugh. "We hardly ever have snow in July and August."

"Something to look forward to, then," she answered, then moved away. She would worry about Trace Bowman and her very inconvenient feelings for him later. For now, she had a shift to finish, responsibilities to meet.

A nest to protect.

* * *

As he sat down with the mayor and listened while Quinn outlined the complaints he'd received about the intersection of Aspen Grove and Skyline Road, Trace couldn't seem to keep himself from watching Becca out of the corner of his gaze.

He found everything about her fascinating, from how she tucked her hair behind her ear, to the way she nibbled on the end of her pencil as she took orders, to the little wrist flip she did as she delivered a customer's order.

He wasn't the only one drawn to her. Because of her quiet dignity and warmth, people just seemed to want to be around her. The old coots who were The Gulch regulars were completely enamored. They flirted and joked and teased. She didn't appear to mind. She flirted right back with them. He imagined just the tips from the breakfast regulars would go far to help her with her budgetary needs.

Soon she made her way through the dining room toward the open table Quinn had found near the hall leading to the bathroom, though she still seemed to be avoiding his gaze.

"Mayor, would you like more coffee?"

"I'm good, thanks."

Finally she met his gaze and he saw wariness there and something else, something that looked like barely veiled panic.

"Chief Bowman, are you ready to order?" she asked, pulling out her notebook and pencil.

The idea of her in a position of servitude bothered him for reasons he couldn't have explained, but he didn't have a choice in this situation. "I'm going to have to go with what works. I'll have my usual. Western omelet and a stack."

"A man who knows what he wants."

"I'm beginning to," he murmured.

Her eyes widened and she stared at him for a long moment. Currents zinged between them and he couldn't believe everybody else in the diner didn't notice. Finally she wrenched her gaze away and nearly stumbled in her haste to escape their table and head toward Lou and the grill to give his order.

"In the short-term, we need a four-way stop there at the minimum, wouldn't you agree?" the mayor said.

Trace turned his attention back to the conversation and responded appropriately, though half his mind was still occupied with Becca and Gabi. A few moments later, he saw her glance at her watch and then head to the girl's table, probably to remind her it was time for school.

Gabi's face was all puckered and tight like she wanted to cry. Poor kid. He didn't blame her for not wanting to go to school. When he had spoken with her earlier, he had mainly intended only to tell her he was relieved she wasn't dying, but the moment she saw him, Gabi had looked even more miserable, if possible. Her features had dissolved into distress and she had stammered out an explanation about wanting to get out of P.E. and the story exploding beyond her control. She was visibly upset and had even apologized to *him* for her deception, when he had merely been a bystander in the whole situation.

He hadn't lectured her. Instead, he had told her about the time he and his twin brother had tried to deceive their teachers by trading places in school and he'd learned later his brother had only come up with the idea so he could get out of three tests he had that day. What had started as a funny joke had turned into the worst day of his young life.

The poor girl had laughed at the story but she was still quite obviously very sorry for what she had done. He'd also given her the benefit of his life experience by telling her things that seem impossible to face are never as hard as they appear. Like yanking a bandage, it was usually better to do it fast and get it over with.

She wouldn't have an easy time of it in school that day but she would get through it.

On some level, he could relate. He knew what it was to regret something with every breath, to wonder how he could ever face the people he had wronged. After his parents' murders, he had expected Caidy and his brothers to hate him for his unwitting part. If he hadn't been so self-absorbed with Lilah Bodine, he would have been at the ranch with his parents. He didn't know if he could have stopped the home invasion robbery but he might have been able to use the negotiation skills he'd gained as an MP to keep the situation from exploding as it had done.

Instead, he'd been drinking and partying, making out with a lying little bitch while his parents died violent and tragic deaths, his younger sister emotionally scarred for life.

His siblings hadn't blamed him. He still didn't understand why but he was deeply grateful for their forbearance. He pushed the thought away as he watched Becca help Gabi into her coat and backpack. He couldn't hear their conversation but he saw Becca pull her daughter into a hug. "I'm sorry, honey, but you have to face this," he heard her say.

Gabi released a heavy sigh and started trudging toward the door as if she were heading toward a month of math exams. She had to pass his table as she went and he impulsively reached out a hand and grabbed her arm. "Everything will be okay, Gabi. Any girl tough enough to set up a Christmas tree on the first try can handle this."

She didn't look convinced but she still gave him a hesitant smile that seemed to reach right in and nestle next to his heart. "Thanks," she said.

"You're welcome."

When he looked up, he found Becca watching him with an unreadable look in her eyes. Just before Gabi reached the door, Becca called out to her to wait for a moment, then she turned to Donna, working behind the counter. "Donna, do you mind if I take my break a little early so I can run Gabi to school? It's snowing pretty hard out there."

"No problem," the older woman answered. "I can cover your section."

Becca hurried to the back room and returned a moment later minus her apron and carrying her coat and purse.

While she was gone, Trace and the mayor finished their plan of attack on the hazardous intersection—a new four-way-stop and better signage—and the mayor excused himself to meet with the head of the public works department that took care of the roads.

Trace was just about done with his omelet when Becca returned, her features tight with stress.

He had a ridiculous urge to pull her down beside

him, tuck her under his arm and let her lean on him for a moment. She gave him a distracted smile but moved into the back room again to change out of her coat and back into her apron.

He needed to head into the station but found himself reluctant to leave without talking to her again. When she bustled out and started making the rounds of the diner with coffee, he fought the urge to grab her hand and make her stop and rest for a moment. Finally she made it to his table.

"Looks like the mayor paid for your breakfast. Would you like more coffee before you leave, Chief Bowman?"

She had called him Trace when he kissed her. He found himself reliving that kiss in great detail and wanting nothing more than another taste. "I'm good. I've got to head into the station, anyway. Gabi made it to school, then?"

Her smile faltered a little and he saw worry in her eyes. "I stayed and watched her walk all the way through the front doors and even saw Jennie Dalton greet her at the entrance. I don't think she'll be able to duck outside again, not with the principal herself in view."

He had a feeling Gabi was clever enough to do just that but he decided not to worry Becca by sharing that particular opinion.

"She told me what you said, about being brave enough to face her lies and how much better she'll feel when she's made things right. Thank you."

"You're welcome. She's a good kid, Becca. I really do think she just told a little lie and then got carried away. It happens."

She opened her mouth to respond, then closed it

again, obviously changing her mind. "I'm sure you're right, Chief," she said solemnly before heading to the kitchen.

The mayor had probably covered his tip as well, but Trace left a few bills on the table anyway, wanting to leave her a healthy but not exorbitant gratuity. She would hate feeling like an object of charity, he knew.

His day was hectic with snow-related trouble. Besides the usual car accidents, a section of roof collapsed on the auto parts store, injuring an employee and a customer. He only had time for the occasional worry for Becca and Gabi until he returned to his own house twelve hours later to find a basket on his doorstep, its contents hidden in red tissue paper.

It wasn't unusual this time of year for Pine Gulch citizens to drop off the occasional thank-you gift for the police department. People typically made these sorts of deliveries to the police station but since everyone in town knew where he lived, he had occasionally been the recipient of a box of fudge or some peanut brittle. He considered that one of the best things about living in Pine Gulch. The small police force had its detractors, certainly, but most of the residents seemed to appreciate the sacrifice and dedication of his officers.

He slid open the envelope and saw the note with its slanting, firm handwriting. "We made sugar cookies this afternoon and Gabi wanted to bring you some," Becca wrote. "Thank you for buoying up a frightened girl. She survived the day, with your help."

He unlocked the door to a barked greeting from his ugly, grumpy dog, who spent most of the day sleeping or sniffing around the perimeter of his yard as if guarding a demilitarized zone.

He patted the dog's head and scratched behind his ears. Poor thing, spending so much time by himself. Trace tried to take him around town whenever he could, but Grunt seemed to prefer his own company, probably from all those years as a companion to a dour old man.

He ought to look around for a new home for Grunt. A family, maybe. Noisy and hectic. That would be good for him. Caidy had offered to take him to the ranch to add to her menagerie. Grunt wasn't crazy about horses and had a hard time keeping up with Caidy's more active ranch dogs, but he might still enjoy the company.

He nibbled on a cookie, then gave a tiny section to Grunt, who gobbled it up and came back looking for more. Trace knew he ought to just sit here and eat his cookies and stay away from his very lovely—and dangerous—neighbor. But he found himself consumed with curiosity to find out how things went for Gabi beyond this hastily penned note.

"Do you want to go for a walk?"

The dog yawned and planted his head down across his front paws. Trace shook his head in exasperation. "Too bad. We're going."

He grabbed the leash off the hook by the door and fastened it around the dog's collar, then surveyed his kitchen. He needed more of an excuse to drop by her house than merely taking his dog for a walk. When his gaze landed on the basket full of cookies, he smiled and reached into the cupboard for another container. After transferring the cookies from her basket to his container, he rummaged through the cupboard for one of his few precious remaining jars of pepper jelly that Caidy and Destry had made him in the summer. They knew it was his favorite, so every year Caidy put up a dozen jars just for him. He cherished each one but he was willing to part with one if it would get him through Becca's door.

By the time he hooked the leash on the dog's collar, Grunt had perked up a bit and shuffled around impatiently for Trace to unlock the door. The snow had stopped, he was glad to see. This had definitely been a record-breaker of a December so far. The snowmobilers were loving it.

Somebody with a snowblower had cleared all the sidewalks on the street, he was grateful to see. He followed the ridged tracks all the way to Wally Taylor's old house. Her curtains were open, and as he approached the house he saw her inside on the sofa, wrapped in a blanket with a book spread open on her lap, a lamp lit beside her and the Christmas tree lights sending shifting colors across her features.

Something hungry and insistent curled low in his gut. He wanted her, wanted this. The whole picture: a cozy fire on a bitter winter's night, a comfortable house made welcoming for the holidays and especially the warm and lovely woman waiting for him at the end of a hard day.

He didn't want these feelings, particularly not for a woman who didn't trust him and who pushed him away at every opportunity, but he was very much afraid it was too late.

She looked up from her book at that precise moment and her gaze met his through the frost-filigree glass of her window. Her eyes widened with surprise and something else. He wanted to think she was happy to see him but he couldn't be sure.

He gestured toward the front door, then walked up

onto the porch to wait for her to open it. When she did, her features were wary.

"Trace! Come in. It's freezing out there."

"I've got my dog. Do you mind if I bring him inside?"

"You have a dog?"

"Well, I've always assumed he's a dog, though he might be a mutant goblin of some sort."

She gazed down at his funny-looking dog with a look of fascination. "He's welcome to come inside."

Warmth enfolded him as he walked inside the house that smelled of Christmas, of pine trees and cookies and cinnamon.

"He's, um, an interesting-looking dog."

"He was your grandfather's, actually. Grunt, this is Becca."

The dog belched a greeting and Becca smiled a little before turning back to Trace. "What kind of dog is, um, Grunt?"

"The vet says French bulldog, mostly, with a few other breeds thrown in just to muddy the waters."

"Ah. Is everything okay? Please don't tell me you just found out Gabi's been spreading some other kind of lie. I don't think I can handle more."

He laughed, though he was thinking again how foolish he had been to come here. "No. Grunt needed to get out so I thought I would return your basket and tell you thanks for the cookies."

"That was all Gabi's idea. She insisted we take some to you."

"We shared one before we walked over and it was delicious. I'm not sure I can eat a dozen sugar Christmas trees on my own but I'll do my best."

She smiled. "I told Gabi it might be too many but she wanted you to have a basketful. You can always take them into the station for the other officers."

"I might do that." He paused and decided he might as well be honest. "Okay, returning your basket was only an excuse. Though I did include some of my prized pepper jelly."

"You make pepper jelly?"

"No. My sister and niece do. But I certainly prize it."

She genuinely laughed at that, something he considered a major accomplishment. "Okay. Why did you need an excuse?"

"I had to know how things went today for Gabi. Did the other girls shun her after she told the truth, that she wasn't sick?"

"No, actually." She returned to her seat on the sofa and he took that as invitation to sit down in the easy chair. Grunt sniffed around the house, probably looking for some lingering trace of his previous master, poor thing. "She said a few of the girls were angry but most of them seemed happy she wasn't really dying. Gabi said their reactions will help her know which girls are really her friends."

"How about Destry? Was she one of the angry ones?"

Becca's expression softened. "Gabi said she was one of the kindest of the girls. She even invited Gabi to a sleepover during the Christmas holidays."

He was grateful he wouldn't have to have a sit-down talk with his niece about compassion and forgiveness. "Des has faced her own rough road. Her mother walked out on her when she was just a toddler and I think that might have made her more compassionate than most kids her age."

"That can happen." She studied him for a long moment. "Are you just coming home from work, then? It's nine o'clock."

This was becoming a habit, seeing her at breakfast and then again at the end of the day. He probably shouldn't find such comfort in that.

"Yeah. It's been a crazy day. Slide-offs and fenderbenders. For some reason, people completely lose all good sense when it snows."

"Did you eat dinner?"

"Not yet. I'll find something when I head home."

"I made soup tonight for dinner. Minestrone and breadsticks. We've got tons of leftovers. If you'd like, I could heat you up a bowl."

His stomach grumbled and he realized he hadn't eaten since breakfast, the last meal she'd served him.

"I didn't come here for you to fix me dinner, Becca."

Why did you come here? She didn't speak the words but he could see the question plainly in her eyes. He hoped she didn't ask, as he wasn't entirely sure he could answer.

"I'm happy to do it. Consider it my little way of helping the police department."

While she headed into the kitchen without waiting for him to answer, he shrugged out of his coat and draped it over a chair. Grunt jumped into Trace's recently vacated chair as if it had been his customary place.

"You miss him, don't you, bud?"

The grouchy dog gave a cross between a whine and a sigh and closed his eyes. Out of sheer curiosity, Trace picked up the thick book she had been reading and just about fell over at the title and the contents.

He carried the heavy legal journal into the kitchen and held it up. "Nice, relaxing reading for a winter's evening."

Her lips parted and her hands froze in the process of spooning soup into a bowl. He thought he saw embarrassment and perhaps a trace of guilt flit across her features. "I'm hoping to be accepted into the Idaho bar in the next few months," she said, almost defiantly. "As part of the process of reciprocal admission, I have to take some self-study classes on Idaho state law and procedures."

He stared at her, completely floored. Everything he thought he knew about her had just been shaken and tossed out the window.

"You're an attorney?"

"Yes. I have been for three years. But I can't technically practice in Idaho until I complete the process."

"What's an Arizona attorney doing slinging hash at a diner in tiny Pine Gulch, Idaho?"

She looked away, focusing her attention on the bowl in front of her. "That's a really long story. Do you want some grated romano cheese in your soup?"

Trace had plenty of experience with evasion in his profession and he knew sometimes the best strategy was to exercise a little patience. "Yes. Thank you."

For the next few moments, he was busy enjoying the very savory and delicious soup, rich in vegetables and broth. She heated up several breadsticks for him and slid them onto a plate, then sat down across the little table from him.

"So what's the story, Becca?" he finally asked.

She sighed. "After my, um, grandfather left me the house, I decided Gabi and I could both use a change. This was a good opportunity for us. That's all."

"*That's* your long story?"

"The CliffsNotes version, anyway."

As he tried to reconcile this new picture of her, he realized the image of her as a lawyer gelled much more clearly in his mind than as a waitress. He knew many very clever and savvy waitresses but he had always sensed Becca didn't quite fit in that venue.

He also was smart enough to figure out there was more to her story than her very brief explanation.

"And Gabi's father? Where does he fit into the story?"

Her eyes flared with shock at the question but she hid it quickly behind a cool smile. "I believe he was just a minor footnote in the introduction. He's not in Gabi's life whatsoever and hasn't been for years."

He was happier about that than he ought to be. "Are you intending to open a practice here?" he asked.

"Eventually. That's the plan, anyway, when I save enough money. I still have some student loans I'm paying off and I'm trying not to go into more debt if I can help it."

He was *definitely* happier about that than he ought to be. Not the debt-paying part, though that was certainly honorable, but the part about her wanting to open a practice in Pine Gulch.

"What sort of law?"

"In Phoenix, I was involved in contract law. Real estate, specifically. I imagine if I want to practice in a small town like Pine Gulch, I'll have to branch out into whatever my clients might need."

He was still having trouble processing all this. "You said you were a real-estate attorney in Phoenix. Were you working for a firm there or did you have your own practice?"

She looked toward the fire, not meeting his gaze. "I was an associate in a large firm."

"Was it tough to walk away from Phoenix? You probably had clients you'd worked with for a while there."

She jumped to her feet and headed to the fire to add a log from the small stack on the hearth. "We needed a new start," she repeated, her voice firm, and again he sensed there was more to the story. Her features were taut with fine-etched tension. She wasn't telling him something. He sensed it instinctively but he could think of no way to persuade her to trust him with her problems.

Grunt whined suddenly, probably wondering why Wally Taylor wasn't the one fueling the fire, why the old man didn't come shuffling out of the kitchen somewhere.

"I can't believe you kept my grandfather's dog," she said with a rueful shake of her head.

"I was afraid the local shelter wouldn't be able to find someone else to adopt him. He's not the most attractive dog."

"I hadn't noticed," she murmured dryly. Ugly dog or not, she walked toward the chair where the dog was now looking mournfully around the room. She scratched him on the scruff and Grunt sniffed her with considerable reserve on his smashed features. He apparently decided she would do because he darted his tongue out and licked her hand, a show of acceptance Trace wasn't sure he'd earned yet.

"He's really quite adorable, in a hideous sort of way."

He gave her a considering look. "Would you and Gabi like to adopt him?" he asked on impulse. "I was just thinking earlier that he needed a house with children in it. Besides that, I'm rarely home and he's alone all day. I think he's lonely and I'm sure he would be happier here in the only house he's ever known."

Shock flickered in her eyes and her gaze shifted from the dog to him and then back to Grunt again. "I...I don't..."

"You don't need to decide right this minute. Think about it. Anyway, it was only an idea. I can always take him out to the ranch. My little sister sort of has a thing for rescuing animals and he might enjoy living with the other dogs."

"I've never had a pet."

"Really? Never? Not even when you were a kid?"

"No. We...we were never in one place long enough to take care of an animal. My father died when I was small and my mom raised me alone. She...moved around a lot."

He found that inexpressibly sad. What sort of childhood must she have endured, always on the go? He felt blessed all over again that his parents had created such a warm and loving home for him in Pine Gulch, full of horses and art and music and unending acceptance.

Maybe that was the reason she had moved here, the chance to give her daughter the stable, comfortable home she'd never had.

"Well, give it some thought. If you think you and Gabi would like to make a home for Grunt here, let me know. He's house-trained and obedient, for the most part. A little on the lazy side but that's not a bad thing in a little dog. He doesn't bark much and despite his unfortunate looks, he's loyal to a fault."

He paused, debating his words before deciding to tell her. "When I found your grandfather, Grunt was stretched out at his feet. I don't think he had moved for that entire twenty-four hours from when Wally died and I found him. First thing he did was run to his water dish and lap up every drop."

She gazed at the dog again, her eyes soft. He saw clear longing there, despite the dog's scrunchy face and permanent scowl, but indecision flickered there, too. "Right now it's all I can do to take care of Gabi, you know? I've been thinking we need to get a cat to take care of the mice. A dog, though. I'm not sure I can add another creature into the mix."

"Maybe when things settle down. I'll keep the offer on the table."

"Thank you."

He rose and Grunt rose with him. "We should probably be going. You and I have both got early days tomorrow. Thank you for the soup and the cookies."

"It's small recompense for all you've done for us since we arrived in Pine Gulch." She was quiet for a moment, then she gave him that rare, full-fledged genuine smile that always seemed to take his breath away. "You've really made us feel welcome, Trace."

"I hope you give Pine Gulch a chance, Becca. It's a nice town. Even for lawyers."

She shook her head, giving Grunt one last pat as Trace shrugged back into his coat.

At the door, he paused and on impulse reached out and folded her fingers in his. "I'm just going to say this, okay? You can take it any way you want but just know that it's sincere. I hope you know that if you're ever in any kind of trouble, you can always come to me."

She blinked, clearly startled. "I...thank you."

"I mean it, Becca." Whatever was putting those shadows in her eyes, that strain in her features, he knew he probably couldn't fix it but he could at least let her know she had somebody else in her corner.

"Thank you," she murmured again.

He should just have grabbed his ugly little dog and headed out into the night. He might have, but then the light in her entry reflected in her eyes and he saw the glimmer of tears there and he was lost.

With that same unrelenting sense of inevitability, he sighed, released Grunt's leash and reached for her. She gasped a little and then settled against him, her body soft and yielding, and he lowered his mouth to hers.

Chapter Ten

Foolish, foolish woman.

She knew better than this. She knew exactly the sort of trouble she was courting by allowing these seductive kisses. She was allowing him inside her life, inside her heart. When she wasn't with him, she was thinking about him. When she *was* with him, she could feel herself falling deeper and deeper.

A ribbon of need seemed to curl and twist around them, wrapping them tightly together. Lovely and sultry, but more dangerous than a pit viper.

She couldn't let her life become more tangled with his. Trace was exactly the wrong man for her. He couldn't have been *more* wrong if Monica had selected him herself.

She was coming to rely on him too much, on his kindness and his friendship, on the heat and wonder of these stolen kisses that seemed to make the world much less scary.

His mouth was warm and firm and he tasted buttery from the breadsticks. She leaned into him, soaking up his strength and his heat, wishing she could stay here all night with him in this delicious embrace and let all the troubles of the world stay outside the door.

He was still wearing his parka, though he hadn't zipped it, and she slid her hands inside, to the heat at his sides. He was like a solid column of muscle, with no ounce of anything but strength.

With his arms around her, she felt…safe, for the first time she could remember.

Was it any wonder she was falling for him? Trace was the kind of man who gave an ugly little dog a home because he worried no one else would. He loved his family, he was dedicated to his community, he was extraordinarily kind to her sister.

The word jarred her back to reality. Her sister. Not her daughter.

That was the critical point. How was she going to tell him that Gabi was her sister after she'd spent weeks lying to him?

She was no better than Gabi. She had perpetrated a fraud on the Archuletas, on Trace, on the whole town of Pine Gulch. When he found out she had lied to him, he would be furious with her. She pictured the warmth in those green eyes changing to cold anger and her stomach twisted.

Though it was the hardest thing she'd ever done, even harder than striking out on her own when she was sixteen and had no money and no place to live, Becca forced herself to slide her mouth from his, to step back a pace. Cool air rushed in to fill the place where his body had been pressed to hers and she shivered but forced herself to be resolute.

"This isn't a good idea, Trace."

He raked a hand through his hair, his breathing ragged and his eyes a warm, dazed green which she refused to find flattering.

"You're right. Not when Gabi is asleep upstairs."

"That's…not what I mean." She shoved her hands in her pockets to keep from reaching for him again, her nails digging into her palms as if that hard, sharp pain could help her stay focused. She hated this, abhorred the idea of hurting him when he had been nothing but kind to her, but she had to do whatever was necessary to discourage him. She had to make it absolutely clear that she didn't want any more of these wondrous kisses.

Somehow she had to pull off the biggest con of her life.

She drew in a sharp breath, ignoring the harsh pain that nestled somewhere under her heart. "Don't kiss me again, Trace," she said, her voice firm even while her insides were trembling. "I meant what I said. I don't want a relationship. Not now. Not with you."

His head jerked back an inch or two as if she'd just slapped him. His gaze met hers and she saw a confused hurt there that made her stomach feel hollow and achy, as if she'd just drop-kicked his ugly little dog in front of him.

"Wow. That's plain enough."

"You're a very nice man, Trace. I obviously find you attractive or I wouldn't have kissed you. But attraction isn't enough. Not for me, not at this stage in my life. You've been a good friend to…to both Gabi and me, but right now that's all I have room for in my life. I don't want to hurt you but it's not fair for me to let you think I might be open for more. I tried to tell you that before."

"Right. You did." He was angry now. She could see it in the flare of his eyes and the hard, implacable set of his jaw. "You told me and I stupidly ignored you."

"You're not stupid. This isn't your fault, Trace."

"*It's about me, not you.* Isn't that what people say when they're giving someone the brush-off."

Oh, she hated this. She wanted nothing but to have those strong arms around her, to press her cheek against that wonderfully solid chest and just hold on tight. But that was impossible, and the best thing for both of them was to make that perfectly clear to him so she wouldn't have to be tempted again and again to throw her good sense into the wind.

"In this case, it's true. It is about me. I'm sorry if you don't want to accept that but I can't change it."

"So that's it. 'Stay away, don't bother me again. Take your dog and get the hell out of here.'"

The pain in her heart spread through her entire chest cavity but she called on every deceptive skill her mother had ever taught her and gave him a hard little smile. "I wouldn't have phrased it exactly like that."

He stared at her for a long moment and she hated seeing that warm light that had been there when they kissed fade into anger and hurt. "I can't argue with that, can I? Come on, Grunt. Let's go home."

He picked up his dog's leash and opened the door. A cold wind blew inside, chilling every part of her that wasn't already icy. He gave her one last look, then walked out into the night, closing the door firmly behind him.

She watched him walk down her steps onto the sidewalk, then turn toward his house at the end of the street. Snow swirled around him. It might have been a trick of the low light from the streetlamp and the pale moon filtering through clouds, but she could swear it increased in fury and intensity as he walked down the street.

Though she was freezing, she couldn't summon the energy to close the door. She stood there in the cold, looking out at the lights glimmering on all their neighbors' houses, her chest aching with a deep sense of loss.

Oh, how she wished things could be different. Why couldn't she have a normal life, with a cozy house— instead of this dark, depressing old place—with a boyfriend and a little dog and a regular job?

Instead she had a sister who might be a pathological liar, a mother who wasn't happy if she wasn't defrauding someone out of considerable amounts of money, and she had just pushed away the most wonderful man she'd ever met because she was worried he would see through her lies.

Would see that she wasn't good enough for him.

There was the truth. Becca pressed a hand to the ache in her stomach. She was afraid in her heart that she was so scarred from her insecure childhood that she had nothing to give a man like Trace Bowman. Otherwise she would have just faced the truth head-on—told Trace about her mother, about the years of lies and pain, about trying to distance herself as much as she possibly could from Monica until that day her mother and sister had shown up in Phoenix. What had she done that was so wrong, really, other than lying to the school and perpetrating a fraud on the town she was trying to make her own?

She shivered, the cold seeping deep into her bones,

and she finally forced herself to shut the door. She had made her choice to push him away and she would live with it. What else could she do?

Now she had to focus on Christmas a few days away, on making the holiday as perfect as she could for a girl who had never known the normal traditions of childhood.

A guy didn't die of a bruised ego. Or a broken heart, come to that.

He wasn't sure which one he was dealing with. Trace only knew that something burned in his chest and a dark mood had settled over him that no amount of holiday cheer could lift.

He sat in his patrol vehicle outside the diner wishing with everything inside him that he didn't have to go inside. He could see her through the half-curtain windows—making conversation, delivering plates, taking orders. She moved with that quiet grace with which she did everything and she looked so beautiful he couldn't seem to look away, like a kid staring into the sun even when he knew damn well it was bad for him.

He would have picked any other place in town to meet with the mayor again about the pesky intersection that apparently the mayor couldn't sleep until they fixed. He had even suggested The Renegade, the tavern on the outskirts of town. Hell, at this point he would have preferred meeting in his patrol car, but the mayor had insisted on The Gulch, much to his dismay. Said he hadn't eaten breakfast and was starving and needed to be seen patronizing local businesses.

Trace didn't want to go inside. He hadn't seen Becca

since Monday night, two nights ago, when she had basically sent him packing. He told himself he hadn't made a conscious effort to avoid her, but in his heart, he knew otherwise. He was avoiding her, pure and simple.

He didn't expect every woman he was interested in to fall madly in love with him. That was ego he simply didn't have. Taft was the womanizer between them, not Trace. But he had sensed something special with Becca. She certainly didn't kiss him like a woman who wanted nothing to do with him.

He obviously had no instincts about this sort of thing. The last woman he had wanted to pursue a serious relationship with had ended up dumping him, too. He'd thought he and Easton were on the brink of falling for each other when Cisco Del Norte came back to Pine Gulch and he realized East was crazy in love with the man.

Becca wasn't Easton Springhill. He wasn't wrong—she was developing feelings for him, just as he was for her. He had sensed it in the way she kissed him, had seen it in her lovely hazel-brown eyes, but for some reason she wouldn't let him inside.

He couldn't help wondering if she was still hung up on Gabi's father, but she had seemed quite clear the night before that the man wasn't in either of their lives and hadn't been for a long time.

He sighed. Didn't matter her reasons. The woman asked him to back off and he had no choice but to accept that. And while he might wish to avoid her for the next, oh, year or two, that was impossible in a small town like Pine Gulch. Like it or not, he was going to have to face her eventually. Might as well get it over with.

With another sigh, he climbed out of his vehicle.

When he pushed open the door to the diner, heads immediately turned to see if the newcomer was anybody interesting. A few people waved, a few deliberately turned away. Being the police chief of a small town didn't always help a guy win any popularity contests, not when he sometimes had to arrest someone's brother or kid or wife. It didn't bother him much anymore.

The mayor wasn't there yet. Damn. That would have eased this awkwardness a little. When Becca saw him, color rose in her cheeks and she faltered a little before she pulled back her shoulders and stepped toward him. She was wearing a little snowflake ribbon in her hair and more snowflakes dangled from her ears, and she gave him a nervous kind of smile.

"Hi. Um, would you like to sit at the counter or a table?"

He frowned. Neither. He'd like to be eating a brown-bag sandwich in his car right now. He forced a casual smile in response. "Table please. The mayor wanted to grab some lunch while we have a quick meeting. He should be here in a minute."

She directed him to an open seat. "Do you need a menu or would you like to wait until the mayor arrives before you order?"

He hated this distance between them and the tension that seemed to seethe and pop like those fizzy fireworks he used to buy on the Fourth of July.

"Coffee?"

"No. Just water, thanks." He really didn't want her waiting on him but didn't see any way around it unless he tried to have a conversation with the mayor at the crowded, noisy counter.

She brought him his water a moment later and he

sipped it, checking his watch about every thirty seconds. He had been there maybe three or four minutes when the front door opened. He looked up, hoping to see Mayor Montgomery. Instead, the stooped, white-haired figure of Agnes Sheffield walked in along with her quieter sister, Violet. The Sheffield sisters were fixtures of Pine Gulch and had lived there for their entire lives. They even married brothers, who were both long dead now.

To his dismay, Agnes spotted him and immediately abandoned her younger sister to stump over toward him, her cane beating a harsh tattoo on the diner's peeled wood floor.

"This is the last straw. I have had enough! You hear me, Chief Bowman?"

Yes, along with the entire diner and probably every storefront on Main Street. "Of course. What's the problem, Mrs. Sheffield?"

"I'll tell you what the problem is. I want an apology, at the very least. An official one, signed on Pine Gulch Police Department letterhead. You're lucky I'm not going to try to take that fool's badge."

"What fool would that be, ma'am?"

"Your officer. Rivera, something or other. Some kind of Mexican name. He gave me a ticket for reckless driving. Me. How absurd is that? I've never driven recklessly in my life, young man."

The woman had needed her keys taken away about three years and two cataract surgeries ago. Her son was a friend of his and Trace knew he should have talked to the man before now and not let the situation degenerate so far. She was becoming a danger to others on the road, and he was going to have to be firm, as difficult as it was.

"It's harassment. That's what it is. I didn't do anything wrong."

"I'll look into it," he promised. "Officer Rivera is a good man, though. None of my officers would give a ticket that wasn't warranted."

"There's always a first time. I say, I did nothing wrong. I might have driven over the yellow line a time or two but I was not weaving. It was snowy. Anybody might have made that mistake."

"But you know you don't see as well as you used to, right?" he asked gently.

Something like fear flickered in her pale blue eyes. He understood it—losing the freedom to remain behind the wheel could be a horrible blow to a woman as proud and independent as Agnes Sheffield.

"That may be, but I can still drive perfectly well."

On impulse, he reached out and took her weathered, wrinkled hand in his. It was cool and trembling. "Mrs. Sheffield. You would hate to cause an accident, wouldn't you? What if you didn't see the school crossing guard and drove through a crosswalk and hurt a child?"

"I wouldn't do that. I'm a fine driver."

"I'm sure you are." He paused. "How about this. After the holidays, you and I can go for a little drive. We can even take Officer Rivera along if you'd like. If you can show us both we're crazy, I'll rip up your citation and get you that apology. On official stationary, I promise."

"And if not?" she asked, her voice small and her tone no longer so truculent.

He squeezed her gnarled fingers. "Then we will just

have to figure out a way to get you around town to the grocery store and your doctor's appointments, okay? Maybe you can let Violet have a turn driving."

"Hmph. We'll see."

The mayor came into the diner before he could answer and greeted Agnes with his customary charm. Trace wasn't sure how he did it, but in about thirty seconds of conversation, Mayor Montgomery had Agnes blushing and tittering like a teenage girl.

He looked up and happened to catch Becca's gaze. She was staring at him with a strange expression in her eyes, something glittery and bright. When they made eye contact, she wrenched her gaze away and headed for their table.

"Mrs. Sheffield, I seated Violet at your favorite table. Mayor, what can I get you to drink?"

The next forty-five minutes were miserable. He forced himself not to stare at Becca every time she came to their table to take their orders or deliver their food. He tried to avoid making eye contact but despite his best efforts, he was aware of her every movement in his peripheral vision Finally they finished the meeting and wrapped up their lunch at about the same time.

"Thanks for meeting me over lunch," Mayor Montgomery said, wiping his mouth with his napkin. "It was the only time I had free today."

"My treat this time," Trace answered. "You paid last time."

"But I invited you."

They wrangled over the bill for a moment but Trace emerged victorious and the mayor excused himself for another meeting. Trace was waiting for the bill when the chimes on the door jangled. From his position facing the door, Trace saw the new customer was a smartly dressed woman in her mid- to late-forties but trying hard to look a couple decades younger. He didn't think he recognized her but there was something vaguely familiar about the shape of her jawline, the angle of her neck.

He was trying to place how he might know her when he suddenly heard a clatter. He turned at the sound and saw Becca staring at the door, broken plates and spilled food at her feet and shock in her eyes.

"Look what you did!" Agnes Sheffield exclaimed.

Becca looked as if somebody had just run her over with a delivery truck. Her features were pale, her eyes hollow and stunned. She stood frozen for a long moment, then seemed to collect herself enough to kneel down and begin cleaning up her mess.

"I'm sorry. I'm so sorry. I'll have Lou replace your food. Oh, did I spill on you?"

She started to wipe off a splatter of sauce from Agnes's sweater, all the while darting little panicky glances at the woman who had come in. Who was it? And why did her presence leave Becca so flustered?

Not his business, he reminded himself, unless the woman was here to stir up trouble in his town. He did feel compelled to help Becca clean up the mess, however.

"Need a hand?" He didn't wait for an answer, simply crouched beside her and started picking up shards of broken plate.

"I just…I need to tell Lou."

Donna approached them with a wet cloth and the mop. "I saw, darlin'. No worries. I've already had him throw another couple of chicken breasts on the grill.

No charge for lunch today, you two," she said to the Sheffield sisters. "And for your trouble, you can have a piece of pie on the house."

"What about one of your sweet rolls instead?" Agnes gave her a crafty look.

"Sure. I can probably find one of those for you," Donna answered.

"A fresh one. It has to be fresh."

"Of course. A fresh sweet roll coming up, Mrs. Sheffield."

"They ought to fire that girl if she can't handle a tray," he heard Agnes grumble to her sister, and he saw that Becca's leached-out color had been replaced by a pale pink as she cleaned up the mess.

"I can do this," she muttered to him.

"And I can help," he said simply. "Is everything all right?"

She met his gaze and he watched as she seemed to become calm and composed right in front of his eyes. He found her skill at locking away all her emotions quite remarkable, though he could still see a shadow in her eyes and he didn't miss the way she completely avoided looking at the newcomer, whom Donna was trying to seat at the counter.

"Everything's great," Becca muttered. "Couldn't be better. I don't know why I'm so clumsy this afternoon. I guess it's just already been a long day. I've been on my feet since six-thirty."

He might almost believe her if he hadn't seen that moment of panic in her eyes and her determined efforts not to pay any attention to the woman who had come in.

When they finished cleaning up the mess, she forced

a smile. "Thank you. I forgot you were still waiting for your bill. Just give me a moment and we'll get you on your way."

She rose in one fluid motion and headed to the kitchen, taking the soiled tray with her. Donna had seated the other woman at a table across the diner from him. He was tempted to go over and introduce himself but thought that might not be wine, under the circumstances.

When Becca returned, she handed him his and the mayor's bill with another distracted smile that didn't come close to reaching her eyes, then she headed toward the woman.

He expected her to hand the woman a menu. Instead, Becca slid into the booth across from her. He had the right cash to cover the bill and could have just left it on the table, but he was too curious to see how this drama would play out. As he watched, Becca and the other woman spent a few moments of intense conversation, but with the general hubbub of the diner, he couldn't hear the conversation. Becca looked to him angry and frustrated but the other woman didn't appear to care much.

Who was she? Why did she seem so familiar to him, like a book he was almost certain he'd picked up once at the library? And why was Becca so upset to see her?

After perhaps a five minutes' conversation, he saw Becca's hands flutter to her jeans pocket. She seemed indecisive, her features tight with frustration, but finally she pulled out a keychain and extracted a single key, which she slid across the table to the other woman almost defiantly.

The woman gave a tiny, triumphant sort of self-satisfied smile that immediately set Trace's teeth on edge as she palmed the key. She slid out of the booth, kissed Becca's cheek and left the diner without ordering anything. Becca sat there for a moment, her features hollow and raw. He very much wanted to go to her, to ask her to tell him what was so terribly wrong, to promise her he would send the woman packing from his town if her presence bothered Becca so much.

Not that he could do such a thing, but he would have liked the chance to try.

As he watched, she smoothed her hands down her apron and stood almost defiantly, lifting her chin and returning to work.

She stopped at two other tables to check on customers before she worked her way to his. "Did you need dessert or anything?"

"I'm good. Thank you." Despite years of training and practical experience questioning suspects and witnesses, he couldn't come up with a clever way to ask her about what had just happened, so he ended up just blurting it out. "Who was your friend?"

"My...friend?"

"The woman you just gave your house key to."

She raised an eyebrow. "Am I under police surveillance now?"

He refused to let her bait him. "I tend to observe things around me. It's part of being a police officer. She obviously upset you."

"She didn't upset me. I was just...surprised to see her, that's all. That was my dear mother, here to spend the holidays with Gabi and me. Isn't that wonderful?"

Her cool tone of voice left him in no doubt the development was anything *but* wonderful to Becca. Her mother. That was why the woman seemed familiar, because he saw traces of her in the woman he was coming to lo— His mind jerked away from the word like a skittish horse at a rattlesnake pit. He saw pale traces of her in Becca.

"That will be nice for Gabi, to have her grandmother around."

"Won't it?" she said mechanically, then turned to leave. Though he knew it was crazy, he reached out and touched her arm. She trembled a little but at least she didn't jerk her hand away.

"I know I've said this before but I just want to repeat that you can come to me for any reason. No strings, Becca."

Their eyes met and he thought he saw a glimmer of yearning there before she became composed once more.

"Why would I need to do that?" she asked with that cool smile he was beginning to hate, then she headed away to attend to another customer.

Chapter Eleven

Monica. Here. In Pine Gulch.

Becca couldn't think straight, barely aware of what she was doing for the rest of her shift as she took orders, bused tables, poured drinks.

How had her mother found them? Becca hadn't discovered the inheritance from her grandfather until after Monica had left, and she had been very careful to cover their tracks. She had been vague and closemouthed with her former coworkers and neighbors about where they were going.

She had feared this very thing. Monica couldn't have anything good in mind to show up out of the blue like this. What could she possibly want? Would she dare try running one of her schemes here in Pine Gulch? Years of experience had taught her she couldn't put anything past her mother. If there was any sort of illicit money to be made in Pine Gulch, Monica would find a way to get in on the action.

She couldn't let her. Becca fought down her panic attack. If Monica started bilking the people of Pine Gulch out of their hard-earned savings, she and Gabi would have nowhere else to go.

She so wished she'd been able to send her mother packing when she showed up at the diner—which begged another question. Of all the places she might have shown up in town, how did she know Becca worked at the diner in town?

Monica *had* shown up, though, and told her she needed a place to stay. Becca had wanted nothing more than to tell her mother to go to hell. The words had hovered there on her tongue. She had almost said them but then Monica had given her an arch look.

"I saw a police car out there. Who does it belong to?" She had scanned the diner and her gaze had landed unerringly on Trace. Monica could spot a cop with a spooky kind of skill. "That handsome devil with the dark hair and those delicious green eyes, right? He's not in uniform. What is he? A detective?"

She hadn't wanted to answer but she knew Monica would probe until she did. "The police chief," she had muttered.

"Ahhh. Perfect. What would that gorgeous police chief do if I walked over and told him you kidnapped my daughter? I can make it a very convincing story. You know that."

Even as cold fear gripped her stomach, she had let her mother goad her into losing her temper. In retrospect, that had been ridiculous but she seemed to have very little control when it came to Monica.

"I didn't kidnap anyone!" she had snapped. "You left

her with me and took off without a word. What was I supposed to do?"

"I never expected you to leave Arizona with her. I don't believe I gave any such permission."

Though the rational part of her knew perfectly well her mother wouldn't want to bring unnecessary attention to herself by reporting a completely nonexistent crime when she had plenty of real crimes that could be pinned on her, Becca had reacted.

"What do you want?" she had hissed.

Monica shrugged. "Nothing so terrible, darling, I promise. Just a place to stay for a few days. I want to spend Christmas with my daughters. Family, that's what the holidays are all about, right?"

The very idea nauseated her, but at the time she had been desperate to get Monica out of the diner. In the end, she had caved and given her mother the key to her grandfather's house.

She would be there now. Picking through her things, assessing their humble Christmas decorations. Probably looking for any weakness in Becca that she could use to her advantage somehow.

Now what was she supposed to do?

She had never been so relieved when her shift ended and Donna told her to go home. She hung up her apron and grabbed her coat off the hook, then drove home as quickly as she dared through the snowy streets of Pine Gulch. In her mind, she rehearsed a dozen ways she would send Monica packing.

She found her mother in the kitchen wearing the frilly pink apron Becca had won at a bridal shower for a coworker in Arizona, what seemed another lifetime ago. She was stirring something in a bowl while Christmas music played on the kitchen radio.

Becca narrowed her gaze. "What are you doing?"

"I thought I would make some peanut butter cookies. They were always your favorite and my Gabi loves them, too."

She had absolutely no recollection of her mother ever making cookies. "How did you find us?" she demanded.

As she might have expected, Monica ignored the question. "How can you stand all that snow? Oh, I'll admit it's lovely for a day or two but I can't imagine putting up with it for months at a time."

Fitting, she supposed. Her mother didn't like to be inconvenienced by anything. Weather, finances, pesky little things like, oh, morals, ethics and laws.

"Tell me the truth, Monica. What are you doing here? I'm not buying the whole 'holiday time with the family' line. What else is going on?"

"Why do I have to have an ulterior motive, darling? I missed my little Gabi. And you, of course." She smiled as she added vanilla to the dough.

"Gabi's fine. She's happy." *She doesn't need you coming in and screwing everything up.*

"Is she?"

Just those two words and suddenly everything became clear. She stared at her mother, those nerves clutching her stomach again. "She found a way to call you, didn't she?"

Monica opened her mouth as if to deny it and then must have decided she could work the truth to her advantage somehow. "Apparently, she borrowed the cell phone of a little friend from school."

Of course. The day Becca had found out about her

claiming she had a heart condition, she'd had an iPod and phone and other electronic gadgetry. Gabi must have known Becca would have figured it out if she'd somehow sneaked her cell phone to use it, so she'd figured out a work-around.

"Gabi knows that no matter where I am or what I might be doing, I've got one cell number she can always use to reach me in an emergency. She called me last week and told me where she was and of course I dropped everything to rush right here."

Her sister was nine years old, she reminded herself. She didn't know any other life than the twisted one Monica had provided for those years. Still, Becca was aware of a sharp ache in her chest. "You left her with me, Monica. You used me and embroiled me in mortgage fraud and cleared out my savings and then you took off. I had no choice but to clean things up the best way I could. I might have been disbarred."

"You weren't, were you?"

"By a *miracle*. Because I agreed to liquidate every asset I had to cover what you stole!"

Monica's smile was conciliatory. "I'll make it up to you. You know I'm good for it, right?"

Oh, of course she would make it up. Like all the other money she had taken from her over the years in one form or another. Becca wasn't going to hold her breath over that particular promise.

"I don't want you here. Neither does Gabi. She's finally got a comfortable, stable home. Someone willing to think about her first."

Monica sniffed. "You call this place comfortable? It's horrible!"

Though she had thought the very same thing herself

throughout the past month, decrying the layers of dark, unattractive wallpaper, the peeling linoleum, Becca suddenly wanted to defend her grandfather's house. This house had provided a haven for them when they hadn't had anywhere else to go and she didn't want to hear Monica malign it.

"There's nothing wrong with this house that a little tender loving can't take care of. We're working on it, little by little. Anyway, that's not the point. The point is, Gabi is fine here. You showing up like this out of the blue will only confuse her."

"She called me," Monica pointed out once more.

"That doesn't matter. Gabi—" *Is here,* she realized, her words cut off by the sound of the front door slamming. School was on an early schedule because Christmas vacation started the next day, she remembered.

"Whose car is out there?" Gabi called from the entry. Becca didn't have a chance to answer before her sister wandered into the kitchen. She stood in the doorway, her jaw sagging at the sight of their mother in an apron, spooning batter onto a cookie sheet.

"Mom?"

"Darling!" Monica took a moment to wipe her hands on a cloth, then rushed to Gabi and enfolded her in a huge hug. Gabi didn't return the hug. She merely stood still, arms at her side.

"What are you doing here?" she asked stiffly.

"You called me, honey. You told me where you were. I thought that meant you wanted me here."

Gabi shot a quick look at Becca, her eyes stricken. "I only wanted to make sure you were okay and let you know we were fine here. I didn't want you to worry. I never thought you would come out here."

"It's Christmas. Where else would I be than with my beautiful girls?"

Becca barely restrained herself from rolling her eyes. She hadn't spent Christmas with her mother in a dozen years. Even when she lived with Monica, her mother had never made any sort of fuss about Christmas.

"We're going to have a wonderful time, darling. We can sing carols and, look, I'm making cookies, and I can be here when you open your presents from Santa. Aren't you so happy that we can be together?"

"Um. Sure," Gabi said. She had that closed-up expression again that always worried Becca.

The rest of the afternoon and evening passed in a stilted awkwardness, with Monica showing over-the-top enthusiasm for everything except the house. She *loved* the snowflakes Gabi had made. She *adored* their humble paper-chain garland. She couldn't get enough of the stockings Becca and Gabi had made out of felt pieces clumsily stitched together.

She apparently didn't notice—or care—that neither of them shared her enthusiasm.

Becca didn't have a chance to talk with Gabi alone until after dinner, when Monica headed to the third bedroom—sniffing her nose at the twin bed and the boxes piled around her that Becca hadn't had a chance to organize yet—to make some phone calls. Gabi immediately headed into the shower as if she wanted to avoid questions. Becca waited several moments after she heard the water shut off for her sister to change into her pajamas before seeking her out.

To her surprise, she found Gabi on the floor of the darkened living room, lit only by the light from the Christmas tree Trace had brought and decorated with them.

Colored streaks dripped down Gabi's cheeks, the Christmas lights reflecting her tears.

"Oh, honey." Becca folded her sister in her arms, marveling anew how she could come to care so much for Gabi in a few months. Gabi was stiff and unyielding for a moment and then she sagged in her arms. A lump rose in Becca's throat when Gabi wrapped her arms around her, too.

"I've ruined everything," she said, sniffling. "I'm sorry, Beck. I never *ever* thought she would come out here."

She smoothed a hand over Gabi's damp hair. "It's not your fault. Monica likes the unexpected. She always has."

"I should never have called her."

She couldn't lie to the girl, after she had known a lifetime of dishonesty, by pretending everything was fine. "It certainly complicates things. But we'll be okay."

"She's going to ruin Christmas."

"Not if we don't let her."

"You promise?"

The trust in Gabi's voice staggered her, left her feeling completely unworthy. She hugged her tightly. "I promise," she answered, though she had absolutely no idea how she was going to keep her word.

Monica was definitely up to something.

Less than twenty-four hours after her mother had blown into town like a nasty, greasy rain cloud, Becca knew she was cooking up some new scheme. Monica was on her cell phone constantly and she insisted on taking every call in the guest bedroom amid the boxes and clutter where she couldn't be overheard.

She also had an unmistakable air of restless excitement around her. Most worrisome of all, she seemed especially watchful of Gabi. At odd moments, Becca would find her mother scrutinizing her sister with a considering expression that worried her to no end. If she caught Becca looking at her, Monica would revert to a bland smile that didn't fool either of them.

Becca had never felt so helpless, trapped by her quandary. She wanted to tell her mother to leave, that she wouldn't let her ruin Gabi's first real Christmas. But with no legal, official custody arrangement between them, she knew Monica could drive away with Gabi at any moment and Becca would have no power to stop her.

She had been so worried, she had almost called in sick that day at the diner, but she knew that wouldn't have been fair to Lou and Donna. The Gulch was bound to be busier than usual this close to Christmas, especially with school out for Christmas vacation. She just had to trust that Monica wouldn't do anything stupid—which seemed a little like hoping Mother Nature would decide to send a heat wave to Pine Gulch for Christmas.

Now, as she pulled into her driveway behind Monica's flashy red sports car, relief flooded her. Her mother and Gabi were still here.

If nothing else, her mother's reappearance in their lives had proved without question to Becca how very much she loved her sister. She didn't know exactly when her perception had changed, but she no longer considered her sister a burden. She loved Gabi and wanted, above all, to give her sister a safe, normal childhood.

A nine-year-old girl ought to be busy going to birthday parties and dance class, not playing a part in her mother's latest con.

If Monica took Gabi away, Becca knew just what fate awaited her. More lies and manipulation. Gabi would have to become a player, willing or not, in whatever game Monica wanted to embroil her in next.

Becca refused to let that happen. She had given her word and she would do whatever it took to keep that promise.

The afternoon and evening were a repeat of the awkwardness of the day before. Though she did her best to keep her sister busy in the kitchen making homemade caramels she wanted to give to the Archuletas and The Gulch regulars the next day on Christmas Eve, Monica still managed to sneak Gabi away for a couple of private talks. Each time, Gabi would return subdued but she refused to talk about what was bothering her with Becca.

After they finished wrapping the caramels in little sections of waxed paper, Gabi finally said she was tired and wanted to go to bed. Though it was about an hour earlier than her usual bedtime, Becca didn't stop her as she headed upstairs to her bedroom.

"Well, I've got to make a few phone calls," Monica said, pushing away from the table, where she had sat and watched Gabi and Becca wrap the caramels.

"Before you do, I need to talk to you." Becca forced her voice to be forceful, declarative.

Monica gave a light laugh, though she seemed slightly disconcerted. "That sounds ominous. You mind if I eat a caramel while you lecture me?"

Without waiting for an answer, she unwrapped one of the sticky-sweet pieces of candy and began to chew it.

"I don't want to lecture you," Becca said. True enough. She wanted to wring her mother's neck for coming here and stirring up such tension, taking so much of the joy out of the holidays. "I want the truth. What are you planning with Gabi?"

Monica opened her mouth with a look of feigned hurt. She could have made a good living in Hollywood if she'd turned her talents in that direction. She was a brilliant actress, which was why she was so good at convincing people to part with their money, whether they wanted to or not.

"I'm not sure what you mean."

"I'm not stupid, Monica. I know the signs. You're cooking up something and it involves Gabi."

"Why would you say that to me?"

Becca ground her back teeth, refusing to play the game. "Because I know you. You forget, I was exactly in Gabi's shoes until I cut off ties with you twelve years ago. Enough is enough, Monica. Gabi and I are making a good life here. She's got friends, she's starting to enjoy school. I'm thinking about getting a dog and a cat. She's safe and happy now, for once in her life, and I'm not letting you drag her off again."

Oh, she should have just shut up while she was ahead. As soon as she said the last part, she wanted to clamp her teeth together at her own stupid tactical error.

Big mistake, to throw everything out there like that and reveal how very protective she was of Gabi now. Monica would definitely capitalize on her mistake. She would have been much better off pretending she didn't want Gabi around. Monica would have been much quicker to leave the girl with Becca if she thought it was some kind of onerous burden on her.

"You're imagining things." Monica put on her wounded look. "I don't know why you're always so quick to accuse me of things. I'm just here to spend the holidays with my girls."

Becca hated to ask but felt she had no choice. "You're not planning something here, are you?"

Monica's look of surprise seemed genuine enough. "In Pine Gulch? No. I learned my lesson here."

She stared. "What does that mean?"

"I haven't had good experiences in Pine Gulch. After your father died, I contacted your grandfather looking for help." Her mouth pursed and she looked every one of her nearly fifty years. "He threatened to take you away from me, the old bastard. I wasn't going to let that happen so I vowed not to come back. When I was pregnant with Gabi, some old acquaintances needed another player for a big job here. The payoff was going to be huge but the whole job turned into a complete disaster. Fortunately I only had a small part. Nobody could tie me to anything. All I did was a little recon work for a few days. It wasn't easy, I'll tell you that, and I was able to get out of town fast when things headed south. You know how I feel about violence. Just not my scene."

She wasn't interested in Monica's walks down Memory Lane. All she wanted was to protect her sister.

"Gabi is happy here," she repeated. "Don't you think she deserves a chance at a normal life?"

"Gabrielle is not you, Rebecca. All you ever wanted was that *normal* you're always going on about. Look at you now. Waiting tables in a two-bit diner in Nowhere, Idaho. I can't believe any daughter of mine would be happy, but I never did understand you. Now, Gabi. She loves adventure."

"She's happy here," she repeated to Monica.

Her mother smiled, tossing her waxed paper wrapper on the counter instead of the garbage can. "If that was true, she never would have called me. Good night, my dear. Sleep well."

She walked out of the kitchen, leaving Becca with more of her messes to clean up and an ache of fear in her stomach.

Chapter Twelve

The next morning, Christmas Eve, The Gulch was only open for breakfast and shortened lunch hours. Becca handed out her caramels and was delighted with the enthusiastic response. Much to her surprise, several of the regulars had little gifts for her, as well—a box of chocolate mints, a plate of cookies, a mug filled with hot cocoa packets. Donna and Lou left a wrapped gift for her on the shelf above where she hung her purse and coat.

Pine Gulch was a nice town, she thought. People here had gone far out of their way to make her feel welcome and she wouldn't soon forget it.

Her happy holiday glow lasted until a little after nine when the door opened and the police chief of this nice town walked in. He was wearing a uniform—something fairly unusual for him, and a PGPD parka and Stetson.

Her traitorous insides trembled, and for an instant,

she fiercely wished things could be different between them—especially that she had been honest from the day she showed up in town about Gabi and Monica. She had an equally fierce wish that Donna wasn't tied up in the office right now so Becca didn't have to deal with him this morning.

"Merry Christmas, Chief. Do you want a table or a booth?"

"Merry Christmas." He gave her a cool nod. "Neither, actually. I just need a sweet roll and a breakfast wrap to go. I've only got a minute before I have to head back on patrol."

"I guess police officers don't get Christmas off."

He shrugged. "I try to give my officers with kids as much time at home as I can during the holidays."

Donna chose that moment to emerge from the back room, more paper place mats in her hand from the storage closet there. "If I know you, Chief, you're going to be working double shifts from now until New Year's."

He shifted, looking embarrassed. "Don't make it a bigger deal than it is, Donna. My officers work hard all year. If I can give them a little more time with their families over the holidays, it's a small enough thing."

Becca gazed at this strong, honorable man, her heart suddenly pounding in her chest. He worked himself into the ground over the holidays, gave up time with his own family, so his officers could be with their children. How could a woman resist a man like that?

She wasn't in danger of falling in love with him, she realized, shock trembling through her. She was already there. She didn't know when it had happened—perhaps that day in the diner when he had protected her from the rowdy snowmobilers or perhaps earlier, when he had shown up at their house with a Christmas tree and that rueful smile.

Or maybe she fell in love when she met her grandfather's dog, Grunt, and discovered Trace was the sort of man who would take in an ugly little dog and give him a home simply because no one else stepped up to do it.

What if she dared tell him the truth? Surely he would understand and forgive her? She had to believe that. After all, she had only been trying to protect her sister.

While Lou fixed Trace's breakfast burrito, she grabbed one of the diner's famous cinnamon rolls from the double batch he had prepared that morning and slipped it into a sack. On impulse, she hurried to the back room for the last small gift bag full of caramels. She already knew Trace had a sweet tooth. Maybe a little candy would help make his long shift a little more bearable.

She was heading back to the dining room when her cell phone rang. Though she carried it with her, very few people had the new number she had obtained when she moved to Pine Gulch. A quick glance at her caller ID verified the call was from her mother's phone. For a moment, she was tempted to shut off the phone and not accept the call. But since Monica was with Gabi, there was always a chance it was some sort of emergency.

"Yes. Hello?" she finally answered, pitching her voice low.

"She's packing my stuff!"

Instead of her mother's voice, she heard Gabi's and the frantic words turned her insides to ice.

"What?" She could only pray she had misunderstood.

"She just went to the bathroom and I sneaked her

phone so I could call you. She's packing all my stuff. I think she's trying to leave before you get back."

Panic exploded through her. She had suspected this very thing, damn it. Why hadn't she brought Gabi to work with her? When would she ever learn that she couldn't trust Monica for a single second? "It's Christmas Eve!"

"I know." Gabi's voice wobbled. "I tried to tell her that we should wait until after the holidays, but she said we need to go, that she has people waiting in California, a man, and she's told him all about me. I've apparently been away at boarding school and now I get to spend Christmas with them."

No. No, no, *no!* She wouldn't let this happen. What could she do?

Feeling wild, trapped, she gazed out at the diner trying to formulate a plan and her gaze landed on Trace looking big and solid and reassuring as he stood at the counter talking to Donna.

Trace. *I hope you know that if you're ever in any kind of trouble, you can always come to me,* he had said to her.

She had to tell him. He was the only one who could help her. How he would do that, she had no idea, but she had to do whatever necessary to protect her sister.

"Stall her. However you can think of, just stall her, okay?"

Gabi was silent for about three seconds. "I'll try," she finally said, doubt threading through her voice. She was probably wondering whether she had put her trust in the right person. Becca didn't blame her for that.

"Hang in there. Whatever you do, don't let her know

you called me. You'll have to delete the record from her recently dialed calls. Do you know how to do that?"

"I can figure it out." Gabi sounded terribly young suddenly. Young and frightened. "I don't want to go, Becca. I like it here with...with you."

This was a vast outpouring of affection coming from her reserved little sister and Becca had to swallow down tears. "I know, sweetheart. I'm not going to let her do this. Your place is here with me now. Hang on, okay? Just stall her."

"Okay. I've got to go. I just heard the toilet flush."

Gabi ended the call and Becca drew a deep breath. After the next few moments, everything was going to be different. The time for lies and deception was over. Trace might hate her now but she couldn't worry about that.

She had to protect her sister, whatever the cost.

He had to stop coming in here.

He would just have to leave enough time in the mornings so that he could make his own breakfast at home before he left for the day or else somehow force himself to be content with a breakfast sandwich from the fast-food place at the other end of town.

It was too hard to come to The Gulch now with Becca here. Every time he saw her, he had to fight with everything inside him not to pull her into his arms and not let go.

"Here's your breakfast burrito. I don't know where Becca has run off to," Donna said, her dark eyes exasperated. "I swear she was putting a cinnamon roll into a bag for you. Let me just grab you another one."

"I saw her go to the back room a minute ago," he

said. Of course he hadn't missed that. He was aware of every move she made, pathetic lovestruck fool that he was.

"I'll just see what's going on," Donna started to say, but before she could move, Becca walked back into the room.

Something was terribly, terribly wrong.

He saw tension in every line of her body, from the tight set of her shoulders to her clenched fists, and her features were as colorless as they'd been that day her mother came into the diner.

She seemed to take a deep breath and then headed toward him. As she neared, he saw fear in her eyes, stark and cold. He instinctively reached his fingers toward his weapon, hovering there—braced for trouble, despite not knowing its source.

"What's wrong?"

She let out a shaky breath. "I need your help, Trace."

"You've got it," he said without hesitation.

She blinked, confusion in her eyes, as if she hadn't expected such ready willingness. Becca struck him as someone who had been carrying her troubles by herself for entirely too long. Maybe it was time she allowed someone else to lend a shoulder.

Her features softened, her mouth trembling, then she pressed her lips together. "I have to tell you something first. You won't like it."

"Sit down first. You look like you're going to fall over."

"I can't. There's no time. I need to…" She drew in a deep breath, her hands in tight fists at her side. "I just have to come right out and say this. Gabi isn't really my daughter."

He stared, the air leaving him a whoosh. He didn't know what to think, trying to process the shock of this revelation.

"It's a long story, one I don't have time to get into right now, but she's really my younger sister. Half sister, I guess. We share a mother. You met her the other day here at The Gulch."

Suddenly so much made sense—her protectiveness about Gabi, the vagueness about their past life together, those few times when Becca had seemed completely out of her element when it came to child-rearing.

"You were surprised to see your mother," he said. He had a thousand questions but that thought seemed to take precedence. "Surprised and not pleased."

"An understatement." Becca rubbed a hand over her face. "A few months ago, she dumped Gabi on me in Arizona and took off without a word. I had no idea where she was or how to reach her, which is usually the way I prefer the situation. But here she is again, out of the blue, and she wants to take Gabi away. We have to stop her."

He felt as if he had missed a step somewhere. There had to be more to this story than a difficult relationship with her mother. He was able to key in on the legalities, however. "You said she's the girl's mother. How can you stop her from taking her? Do you have official guardianship of Gabi?"

"No. I told you, she just dumped her on me. I have no formal custody whatsoever, which is why I thought it would be easier when we moved here to just say she was my daughter." She glanced at her watch. "Custody or not, I have to do something. Gabi doesn't want to go with Monica. She's finally got a home and security, friends at school. She's happy here. If Monica takes her, she'll…" Her voice trailed off and he sensed *this* was the crux of the whole situation, though he didn't know what led him to that conclusion.

"She'll what?"

She said nothing, looking at the floor, the other customers, the counter—anywhere but at him.

"Help me understand, Becca. What's so terrible about a mother wanting to be with her own daughter?"

"Monica doesn't want Gabi." Bitterness seeped from her words. "She only wants to use her in whatever scheme she's cooking up now."

"Scheme?"

She sighed and finally met his gaze, and he saw a lifetime of hurt there. "My mother is a con artist and a thief. She has spent her entire life using everyone around her. I became an emancipated minor when I was sixteen and severed all ties with her because I couldn't deal with the manipulation and lies anymore. I didn't even know about Gabi until a few months ago when my mother showed up in Phoenix with her. I hate myself when I think that. Because I refused to have anything to do with Monica, Gabi spent nine years with her. If I'd known, I might have been able to do something to help her get away years earlier."

She released a long breath. "I wasn't there for all that time, Trace. But I'm here now and I've promised Gabi I won't let Monica take her. Please, can you help me?"

He couldn't see a clear way to accomplish that particular job given the legal parameters of his position, but he wasn't prepared to admit that to her yet. "Can you prove your mother—Monica—is up to something in Pine Gulch?"

"No. Gabi said she's going to California." She frowned. "I think she was involved in a job here once. Years ago. She said something about everything going wrong. I don't see how that can help us, though."

She checked her watch again. "We have to hurry, Trace. She could be driving away right now. Please, will you help me stop her?"

He had nearly felt as helpless as he considered the best course of action. "Without evidence of wrongdoing, I can't just storm in and take your sister away from her mother. I wish it were that simple."

"So you're not going to help me. She's going to destroy Gabi's childhood just like she did…"

"Yours?"

In one short, tense conversation, so many things about Becca seemed vividly clear to him now. She was a series of layers, complex and mysterious. A challenge he found eminently intriguing.

At the core, though, was a woman trying to do the right thing for a young girl. If he could, he vowed he would figure out a way to help her.

"I can stall her," he finally said. "Maybe take her in for questioning on some open cases we have here while we bring in CPD. You said she was involved in something around here years ago?"

"She wouldn't talk much about it, only to say it turned violent unexpectedly and she left when she could. She said her part was small. I will say this for my mother, amoral she might be but she abhors violence. Says it's unnecessary and messy."

He frowned, a little niggle of unease lodging in his gut. "How long ago?"

"I'm not sure, exactly. I had nothing to do with her

for the last dozen years. She did say she was pregnant with Gabi, so that would have been about a decade ago. Somewhere in there. Her job was reconnaissance."

Was it possible that Becca's mother had been involved with the men who had killed his parents? He and the local authorities had been convinced more people had been involved than just the two men Caidy had seen shoot his parents and the woman who had been sent to distract him from coming home in the middle of the robbery.

He felt a little stir of anticipation at the possibility of a break in the case, a link to the people who had killed his parents. At the same time, he didn't miss the irony—he was in love with a woman who just might be the daughter of someone involved in that heinous crime.

He wouldn't worry about that right now, until he met the woman and had a chance to assess the situation.

"I need to go. I can't just stand here." Becca twisted her hands together. "Gabi said Monica is packing her things."

"Grab your coat. Let's go."

Her eyes widened with a dazed sort of shock as if she hadn't let herself believe he would truly help her. This only served to reinforce his belief that she had known very few people she could count on in her life. It made him sad, made him want to tuck her against his heart and promise her he would always be there when she needed him.

"I have to tell Donna."

"I heard, darlin'." The older woman stood a few feet away.

"All of it?" Becca looked worried, probably certain

she would face censure for lying, but Donna stepped forward and squeezed her hands. "You go do what you have to in order to protect that little girl. We'll be fine. I can handle things here."

Eyes brimming with tears she didn't shed, Becca hugged her employer tightly for a moment, then left the room to grab her coat.

"I mean it," Donna said to him when Becca was out of earshot. "You do whatever you have to, Trace. She loves that girl, daughter or not. It sounds like this mother is a real piece of work. You teach her that in Pine Gulch, we take care of our own."

Oh, no pressure. Trace sighed. He would do what he could. But right now his options when it came to keeping a mother away from her child seemed pitifully inadequate.

He was helping her. Some part of her almost couldn't believe this wasn't some kind of trick, that he wasn't going to just take her to the police station and charge her with lying to a police officer or obstruction of justice.

Across the width of the vehicle, Trace watched the road and the tiny snowflakes fluttering down in front of the vehicle. He looked grim and dangerous, his jaw firm and his mouth hard—definitely not a man she would want to mess with under other circumstances. For an instant, she almost felt sorry for Monica for being oblivious as to what havoc was going to rain down on her in a very short time.

She was suddenly very grateful to have Trace Bowman on her side.

He *was* on her side. He had been from the beginning. She had been so stupid not to trust him from the moment she showed up in Pine Gulch. Most of the time she liked to tell herself her tumultuous childhood hadn't left any lasting damage. But once in a while she saw with stark clarity how stunted she was in certain areas. A willingness to allow herself to rely on others was right there at the top of the list. She had been on her own for so long—even before she officially severed ties with Monica—that she had a difficult time giving others any opportunity to see past her defenses in order to help her.

She hadn't expected this sweet, healing relief at knowing someone else was in her corner, helping her fight her own particular dragon.

On impulse, she reached out and touched his arm, feeling the heat and the strength through the thickness of his coat.

"Trace, I shouldn't have lied to you and everyone else about Gabi being my daughter. I'm sorry. When I tried to register her at school, I realized I didn't have a birth certificate or anything. It…seemed easier to say I was her mother than to try to explain the whole messy situation and have to admit I wasn't technically her legal guardian. I was worried the school would have to open an investigation with child protective services. I couldn't bear to think of her being taken away, going into foster care, not when I'm trying my best to give her a comfortable life. Foster care would have been horrible for her."

She'd had a few short bouts in foster care during those times Monica had been arrested and she wouldn't wish that on anyone, especially not the sister she loved.

"I wish you had trusted me."

Her life the last few months would have been so much less stressful if only she hadn't been so stubbornly independent. "I should have."

He sent her a quick look across the vehicle, then turned his attention back to the road as they turned onto the street they shared. "Is that the reason you pushed me away? Because I'm a cop and you were afraid to spend more time with me for fear I would figure it out and take Gabi away?"

"I was raised from an infant not to attract the attention of the police. It's a little hard to break the habit. But yes, that's the main reason."

He said nothing but she thought she saw a glint of something unreadable in his green eyes and then they were at her grandfather's house.

In the driveway, Monica was placing a box in the trunk of her car, which was tricked out with every available luxury.

Trace pulled into the driveway behind her, effectively blocking her escape route. Nicely done, Becca thought, and she watched her mother's features dissolve into a wild, thwarted fury for only an instant before she wiped them clean again.

By the time they climbed out of the patrol vehicle and headed toward Monica in the cold December air, her mother had turned on what Becca always considered her Distressed Maiden persona.

She was very good at what she did. It was always a bit of a surprise to watch the transformation. In the thirty seconds it took them to exit Trace's patrol vehicle, Monica had somehow managed to mess her hair a little like someone flustered and mussed, and transform her features so she looked somehow older, frightened.

"Officer. I'm so glad you're here. You must help me."

Trace raised an eyebrow, looking singularly unmoved. "Must I?"

"Yes. My child is being held here against her will." Her fingers trembled slightly as she pointed at Becca. "She took her away from me and ran off with her. You wouldn't believe how frantic I've been."

"No doubt."

"I've been looking for her for months and now I've finally found her. I've just been waiting for my chance to take her."

"How terrifying for you."

She studied him, apparently trying to decide if he was sarcastic or not but Trace wore no expression.

"Yes, well, I've found her now. We're together again." She offered up a quivery sort of smile. "I don't want to press charges or anything. I just want to take my child and leave your lovely little town."

"Why?"

That single word seemed to stymie Monica. She stared at him for a moment. "Why?"

"Yes. Why? We police types tend to look for motive. It's a bad habit." He gave a self-deprecating little smile that still sent chills down Becca's spine.

In official cop mode, Trace was nothing short of terrifying. Who would have expected the nice man he seemed to be most of the time to be able to come off as such a badass?

"What reason would Ms. Parsons have to take your daughter away from you and move here to Pine Gulch?"

"Spite. Vengeance. She was angry at me because of…some unfortunate real-estate investments and she struck out at me the one way she knew would hurt the most, by keeping my child away from me."

Trace nodded as if he sympathized with her, even accepted the hypothesis. For an instant, Becca felt a clutch of fear. What if he bought Monica's lies? She was extraordinarily good at the con.

No. She reined in the panic. Trace *knew* her. They were friends—and possibly more. He would never believe she would take Gabi out of spite. She had to trust him.

"Why don't we all go inside out of the cold and talk about this?" Trace spoke in a calm-the-situation voice. "Where is Gabi now?"

"Inside packing her things. She can't wait to leave."

Becca stared at her mother, shocked at such a fervent and blatant lie that would be ridiculously easy to disprove simply by asking Gabi. It was not the sort of mistake Monica would normally make, unless she was completely certain Gabi would back up her story. She wouldn't, would she? Gabi had called her, begging her to prevent Monica from taking her.

When they walked inside the house, Gabi was sitting on the floor next to the Christmas tree Trace had brought them. Though it was only midmorning, all the lights on the tree were blazing here in the overcast gloom. Her sister's gaze instantly found Becca's. Instead of her usual cool reserve, Gabi looked frightened.

Becca instantly went to her and pulled her into a hug. This was one of those cherished moments when Gabi didn't resist; she just threw her arms around her sister.

"Doesn't look to me as if she can't wait to leave," Trace commented.

A hint of fury sparked in Monica's eyes again but she

maintained her Distressed Maiden act. "Tell the police officer, Gabrielle. How Rebecca took you away from me and I couldn't find you for months. She brought you here and you've been miserable and can't wait to leave. You called me and begged me to come rescue you. Go ahead and tell him."

Becca felt her sister's withdrawal. Gabi sat up and moved away from her, her thin features pinched. "I called her," she whispered.

Her heart sank. What hold did Monica have on Gabi, beyond the helpless love of a child for her mother? *Oh, sweetheart.*

Trace didn't reveal a hint of his thoughts in his eyes or his expression and she felt that clutch of fear again. With Gabi's apparent corroboration, would he believe that she had taken her sister without Monica's permission?

"Gabi, this is important. I need to know the truth. Do you want to go with your mother?" Trace asked.

The girl's gaze flickered from him to their homespun Christmas tree then to her mother. She completely avoided looking at Becca. She didn't speak, however, merely gave a tiny nod that seared through Becca like acid.

Monica must have convinced her to lie somehow. She remembered Gabi's frightened voice on the phone. *I don't want to go, Becca. I like it here with you.*

Triumph flashed in Monica's perfectly made-up eyes. She smiled at Gabi, who looked even more frightened. "See? I told you! She's been miserable here. Poor thing. It's been a nightmare for the girl. She can't wait to leave!"

She turned on Becca. "I hope you're ashamed of

yourself, trying to keep a child away from her loving mother. I can't imagine how a child I raised could possibly be so heartless. Now if you don't mind moving your vehicle, sir, we'll just be on our way. We've got a long drive ahead of us. I'm sure you understand."

"I do. I believe I understand perfectly." He smiled and those chills skittered down Becca's spine again, "I'm afraid I can't allow you to leave town just yet. I need to make a few phone calls first. I'm sure you understand. Just procedure."

Monica shifted and her careful mask began to slip. "I don't understand. What sort of phone calls?"

"Just technicalities. There's still the matter of your abandonment of your daughter in Arizona."

"Abandonment? I didn't abandon anyone. *She* took her and left town. How was I supposed to find her?"

"You'll have to forgive me but that's the point I'm unclear about. Gabi, how long were you with your sister in Phoenix before you moved here?"

Gabi frowned in confusion. "I don't know. A month, maybe."

"A month. I see. And where was your mother during that time?"

Gabi looked at Becca then at Monica before meeting Trace's gaze. "I don't know. She didn't say. We were staying with Becca in Arizona. And one morning when I woke up, my mom wasn't there. She didn't say anything to me before she left. I waited and waited for her to come back but she never did."

Her sister sounded forlorn, abject. Becca might have thought it was an act, just another masquerade, but she remembered how torn up Gabi had been after Monica left.

"And Becca." Trace directed his attention to her. "Did you have any idea where your mother was during that time?"

She felt a tiny glimmer of hope, like a pale sunbeam just barely piercing through clouds. She understood exactly where he was going with this and she couldn't see at all how Monica could wriggle out. "None whatsoever," she said firmly. "She didn't leave a note or email or try to contact us in any way. The only thing she left was a mountain of debts I ended up having to pay. It took me a month to sell my town house and liquidate what was left of my assets in order for us to move here to the house my grandfather gave me."

Trace gave Monica a long, slow look of appraisal. "Sounds like a fairly cut-and-dried case of child abandonment to me."

Shock held Monica speechless for a long moment. She looked at the three of them as if trying to figure out just where the game had gone wrong. When she spoke, Distressed Maiden had been kicked to the curb. Monica's voice was hard, angry. "Well, I'm here now and I want my child. She said herself she wants to go with me."

"With apologies to Gabi here, I'm afraid it doesn't work that way, ma'am. I'm going to have to take you down to the station with me. We don't deal with this sort of thing very often, so I'm going to have to contact the authorities in Arizona about their particular laws and ordinances. With it being Christmas Eve, that might take longer than normal." He shrugged, just a Good Old Boy frustrated with the system. Apparently the Parsons women weren't the only con artists around.

"It's all going to take time," Trace went on, "but I'm

sure you don't mind. You probably don't have anywhere to be for a few days anyway, do you?"

In that moment, Becca realized with startling, joyful clarity that she was fiercely, crazily in love with Trace Bowman. She wanted to run to him and hug him until her arms ached, to tell him just how perfectly he had handled things from the moment they pulled in.

Gabi had sidled closer to her and reached out to grip her knee. Her sister was afraid to hope, she realized. She knew exactly what that felt like. She covered Gabi's fingers with hers and gave a comforting squeeze.

Monica had apparently decided to try on Angry Power-Broker for size. Her eyes were hard, glittery, her shoulders thrown back. "You are making a serious mistake. You have no idea how much of one. You're crazy if you think I'm going to let some two-bit cop railroad me into some half-assed child abandonment charge that won't stick anyway. I have an excellent attorney and he'll have your badge before we're done with this."

Trace merely gazed back, unfazed. "I look forward to it, ma'am. I truly do. Now would you please put your hands behind your back?"

"You are not going to arrest me."

His smile was lethally sharp. "Watch me."

Much to Becca's shock, he moved behind Monica and grabbed one arm. The metallic clink of his handcuffs sliding on pinged through the room. Gabi made a little sound of distress that caught Trace's attention. He gazed at her younger sister for a long moment, pausing before sliding the other cuff on, then turned back to Monica.

"You know, now that I think about it, there is one more alternative."

"What?" Monica seized on the possibility.

"You sign a legal document giving Becca guardianship of Gabi."

"Forget it!"

He reached for her other arm, handcuff at the ready. "Fine. This way means a lot more paperwork, but it's better than being out in the snow on Christmas Eve anyway. Like I said, it might be a couple of days before I can reach anyone in Arizona but we'll get this straightened out eventually. We might have a few open cases around here we can talk to you about. Oh, say, something that happened ten years ago right around this time of year."

Monica's mouth turned white and she aimed another vicious glare at Becca, looking suddenly years older than her very well–maintained fifty. "I didn't do anything."

"Then you've got nothing to worry about." He sounded cheerful. "We'll sort all that out eventually."

"This isn't right. Trying to take a child from her mother."

He glanced toward the couch, where Becca now sat holding Gabi's hand. "You know, you're absolutely right. Funny thing is, that's exactly what we're trying to avoid here. A woman doesn't necessarily have to give birth to be just the person for the job."

Tears burned in Becca's eyes and she held Gabi's hand more tightly.

The mantel clock chimed ten o'clock. Not even noon and Becca felt as if she'd lived a lifetime since she awoke filled with anticipation for Christmas Eve.

Monica looked at the clock, a hint of panic in her eyes, then she gazed at the sofa at her two daughters. After a long pause, during which Becca could practically see her spinning all the angles, Monica finally released a heavy sigh.

"You're not going to give me a choice, are you?"

"I believe I gave you a choice," Trace said calmly, "Child abandonment charges—and whatever else I can find—or you sign custody over to Becca and leave Pine Gulch."

They all waited, the moments ticking past, until Monica finally frowned. "How am I supposed to sign anything with these stupid cuffs on?"

Gabi hitched in a little breath beside her, her gamine little features a strangely poignant mix of relief and sadness.

"No problem. They weren't locked anyway." He pulled the cuffs off and hooked them on his belt again.

"Becca, you're the attorney. Write up something legally binding that will stand up in court, will you? I can witness as an officer of the court. We still might need to do some maneuvering to dot all the *i*'s, but I have friends on the bench."

Monica looked even more furious at this—probably expecting she eventually could figure out a way to wrangle out of any hasty agreement.

"Let's get this over with, then. I've got places to go."

Fifteen minutes later, it was done. Her quickly composed guardianship transfer was as legally sound as she could make it. Monica signed with short, bitter strokes, then Trace and Gabi unloaded her trunk and backseat. Her mother gave Gabi a tearful hug goodbye, promising to visit as soon as she could. To Becca, Monica only delivered a deep, angry glare, which bothered her not one bit.

Trace backed his patrol car out of the driveway and Monica drove off through the murky December sunlight.

To Becca's surprise, Trace pulled back into the driveway and climbed out.

"You okay, kiddo?" he asked Gabi, whose chin still tended to wobble as she watched her mother drive away. "You didn't mean what you said about wanting to go with her, did you?"

"I only said that because she said she would have Becca put in jail for taking me if I didn't. She's my mom. I love her, even though sometimes it's hard. But things have been better since we've been here. I like going to school and making friends and having my own bedroom." She paused, her features uncertain as she looked at Becca. "Are you sure you want me to stay, though? I've caused a lot of trouble."

"Oh, absolutely, my dear." She hugged her sister close, thinking about how very much her life had changed in a few months. Trace's words seemed to ring through her head. *A woman doesn't necessarily have to give birth to be just the person for the job.*

She hadn't wanted to be a mother before Gabi came into her life. Now she couldn't imagine her world without her funny, clever, challenging little sister.

"I'm going to start putting my things away," Gabi said. "Do you think maybe I could get some posters to hang on the wall?"

Becca fought tears. Gabi wanted to decorate her room, finally, after nearly a month here. "I think that would be just perfect."

With the resiliency of the young, Gabi hurried up the stairs, leaving Trace and Becca alone in her grandfather's living room.

She was suddenly fiercely aware of him, his solid strength and comfort. She remembered the heat of his mouth on hers and the sweet peace she found in his arms.

She swallowed, choosing to focus on the events of the morning instead of those handful of dangerous moments she replayed over and over in her mind.

"Thank you for everything. I can't believe you just let Monica leave like that, without arresting her. What about the old case?"

"The whole point was to convince her to sign the guardianship papers, not to pursue a hazy link to a ten-year-old crime she probably could never be prosecuted for. I would have liked to question her to see if she could lead us to someone else involved, but maybe I can still eventually pursue that."

She stared at him, the pieces falling together finally. Ten years. Pine Gulch. Christmas. A job that went violently wrong. "Your parents. Oh, dear heavens. Do you think she might have been involved with your parents' murders?"

He looked more distant than he had all morning. "Possibly. A woman claiming to be an art student showed up at the house out of the blue a few days before the murders, asking to see the collection. My mother was the only one home. Caidy said my mother told her about it and said she felt sorry for the woman because she was quite pregnant, without a ring on her finger, and seemed tired and down. That's the sort of thing my mother would have worried about. She thought the artwork would cheer her up, so she let her inside to see the collection and take pictures. My mother told Caidy she was quite charming."

Nausea churned in her stomach. "You think that might have been Monica?"

"I don't know. Maybe."

"All the more reason you should have arrested her!"

"I have no proof. Nothing to definitely connect her except a ten-year-old hearsay account of an encounter that may or may not have taken place. It's a starting point, though. A lead I didn't have yesterday."

"I'm so sorry."

"It's not your fault," he said firmly. "You're not responsible for something your mother may or may not have done."

He was absolutely right. She had spent far too much time in her life apologizing for Monica. In Phoenix, she had basically cleaned out her assets to pay Monica's debts. Someone else might have walked away and left the victims to suffer, but that wasn't in her nature. She might not have committed the crimes, but Monica had used Becca's connections in the real-estate world, which left her tangentially responsible.

Trace glanced at the mantel clock. "I should go. We're shorthanded from the holidays and I should be out on patrol."

"Of course. Thank you, again. You've given me a precious gift for Christmas. Peace of mind is better than anything else I could find under the tree."

"I'm glad." He smiled, and for a moment she was lost in the green of his eyes, like new leaves unfurling in the springtime....

She jerked herself back to reality. "I hate to ask but I wondered if I could have one more favor."

"Absolutely."

His immediate willingness sent more warmth to nestle near her heart. "Are you still serious about finding another home for your dog?"

He blinked. "I don't want to give him away," he said slowly. "But I have to think he would be happier where he's not alone all the time."

Wouldn't we all? she thought. "In that case, I think Gabi would love to add Grunt to our family. She's never had a pet before."

"Great! I think you're going to make a dog very happy. And a girl, for that matter. Do you want me to bring him over later so you can give him to her for Christmas morning?"

"What a wonderful idea! I never thought of that."

"I'm on until eleven. Would it be too late for me to bring him over after my shift?"

"Not at all. Are you sure you're okay with giving him away?"

"It will be better for Grunt. He'll be happy to be back here, the place that was the only home he knew. I'll miss his ugly little face but I can always visit, right?"

For some ridiculous reason, she could feel herself blush. "Yes. Anytime you'd like."

"Good to know." He smiled warmly and her blush spread.

"Merry Christmas. I'll stop by later tonight with Grunt."

She nodded and held the door open. Because of him,

her Christmas suddenly seemed wonderfully bright—in no small part because she knew she would see him again in a few hours.

Chapter Thirteen

"I know it's cold. Hang on, little dude. We'll be there in a minute."

Grunt tugged against his leash, his squat legs waddling through snow that reached his barrel chest. The dog seemed to sense he was heading back to his former home as they walked through the moonlit Christmas Eve. He showed more energy and enthusiasm than he had in a long time. Trace had to hurry to keep up, juggling his bundle of blankets and the bag full of food, toys, a water dish.

He had to admit that he was just as eager to reach Becca's house, but he forced himself to take his time and enjoy the cold air, the glitter of stars overhead, the reflection of his neighbors' colored lights gleaming through snow.

All day and evening as he had worked the inevitable fender-benders, grim domestic-disturbance calls, a small kitchen fire at old Mrs. McPurdy's that had resulted in a quick change of venue for her family's annual Christmas Eve bash, he had been aware of a low thrum of anticipation, knowing he would see Becca again.

He hadn't been able to shake the memory of the joy on her face while their mother drove away. Somehow he sensed those moments of sheer relieved joy had been rare in her life and he wanted to give her more.

Yeah, he had it bad.

He sighed, hoping he wasn't jumping ahead of himself here, like Grunt leaping into snowdrifts he couldn't find his way out of again.

The dog gave an excited huff as they reached old Wally Taylor's sidewalk and he started a sideways little dance that made Trace smile. Yes, this would be good for the dog and, he hoped, for Gabi.

The curtains were open again and he could see the Christmas tree he'd brought over a lifetime ago glowing against the winter's night. The scene inside looked bright and warm and infinitely inviting.

He knocked softly on the door, not wanting to wake up Gabi on this night where children found sleep so very difficult.

Becca opened it almost instantly, as if she had been waiting there for him. Her features were soft and welcoming and he wanted to stand on this cold porch all night and just soak her in.

"Hi."

"Hi." He couldn't think what else to say, so he only held up the leash and Grunt pranced through the doorway, the squat, ugly little lord of the manor.

Becca smiled, her eyes bright and happy as she knelt down to scratch Grunt's chin. The little French bulldog gazed at her with complete adoration. "Thank you for bringing him over. Gabi will be so thrilled tomorrow morning when she finds him under the tree."

"He's not the most attractive dog in the world for a nine-year-old girl."

"He's adorably ugly. Trust me, she's going to love him."

Trace reached down to unhook his leash and Grant trotted around the room, sniffing all the corners and the Christmas tree. At least he no longer looked as if he expected to see Wally around every corner.

"Do you want to come in?" she asked.

Yes. With a ferocity that unsettled him. He managed a calm smile. "Sure. Thank you."

She closed the door behind him and he was immediately enveloped in the warmth from the fire and the sweet Christmas smells of pine boughs and cinnamon sugar.

"Let me take your coat," she said.

He shrugged out of it and handed it over to her. Their hands brushed, a tiny spark dancing between them, and he wanted to kiss her with a hunger that bordered on insatiable. She had pushed him away the last time. Would she again?

She hung his coat on the hook by the door. "Can I get you something? Cocoa or tea or something? I'm afraid I don't have anything stronger right now. I should have bought something but I didn't think about it."

"I'm good. Thanks."

They stood in a slightly awkward silence. She was the first to break it, blurting out as if she'd rehearsed it, "I have to say this again. I'm so sorry again about…my mother and Gabi and everything. I feel horrible that I lied to you."

He shook his head. "Please, don't worry about it. I understand why you did. I only wish you had trusted me to help you."

"I should have." She sighed. "From the very first day we met, you've been nothing but…kind to me and to Gabi."

"Kindness has nothing to do with it."

His words sounded harsh, even to his ears. She flashed a quick look at him and he saw awareness bloom there. A fine and delicate tension suddenly seethed between them, and with a low sigh he finally reached for her and kissed her.

After a surprised moment, her mouth softened under his and he felt the brush of her arms at his sides as she wrapped them around him. She fit against him perfectly, her curves in exactly the right places, and she tasted sweet and enticing, a hint of chocolate, a hint of peppermint.

They kissed for a long time and he had the strange sense of familiarity, as if he'd been waiting for just this moment his entire life.

She made a tiny sound of pleasure that slid down his spine as if she'd trailed her fingers there, and her arms tightened around him, pressing her curves against him.

When he lifted his head some time later, her eyes were dazed, her mouth full and so lush he wanted to start all over again at the beginning. He tried to speak and had to clear his throat twice to make any words come out. "I have to know, Becca," he said gruffly. "The last time we were here in this particular place, you told me you weren't interested in a relationship. Does that statement still stand?"

She gazed at him, her eyes a huge, lash-fringed blue. She didn't say anything for several seconds, as if trying to come to a decision, and then she shook her head with a soft smile and stood on tiptoe to kiss him again.

Joy exploded through him and he laughed a little against her mouth, yanking her more tightly toward him. He kissed her hard, fiercely. She responded with a heat and passion that scorched through him, made him want to lower her to the floor right now and forget the world....

He drew in a breath, fighting for control. It was too much, too fast. He wanted to slow things down and savor every moment of this magical heat between them.

With supreme effort, he slid his mouth away, his breathing ragged. They were still standing in her entryway, he realized with some vague sense of surprise. He tugged her with him to the sofa, where he sat down and pulled her alongside him, absorbing her sweetness and her strength and all the things about this particular woman that called so strongly to him.

"It was never about you," she admitted after a moment, wrapped in his arms on the sofa while the fire glowed and the Christmas tree lights flickered.

He was aware of a vast feeling of contentment seeping through him, warming all the cold, empty places he tried not to notice most of the time.

"If you want the truth, I was afraid to let you too close. I sensed, even that first day, that you were a man I could count on, but I just...haven't had very many of those in my life."

He kissed her gently, thinking of how she had walked

such a long, difficult road by herself. He hated imagining her as a girl of sixteen trying to make her way alone in a world that usually wasn't very kind.

By her own strength and force of will, she had carved out a life for herself. Had studied and worked and become an attorney, then had forced herself to give it all up to start over again because of her innate sense of right and wrong.

"I'm here now," he murmured. "And if it's okay with you, I don't plan on going anywhere."

He paused, the words he'd never said to another woman hovering on his tongue. Though some part of him warned caution, he disregarded it. She was the bravest woman he knew. He could at least show a little of that courage. "I might as well get this out there while we're laying our cards on the table. I'm in love with you, Becca."

The echo of his words seemed to hang in the air between them as she stared at him silently for a moment that seemed to drag on forever. Just as he was beginning to think he had spoken too soon, her features seemed to light up from the inside like the sparkle of Christmas lights gleaming under snow—a brilliant, beautiful smile unclouded by worry or stress.

She took his breath away, this woman who had become so vitally important to him.

"That's good," she murmured. "That's, um, really great, since I feel the same way about you."

She kissed him again and he tightened his arms around her, wanting to stay right here for the next, oh, fifty or sixty years. For a start.

She had never dreamed she could be so happy. Joy seemed to pulse through her like her heartbeat, strong and insistent, a beautiful comfort. Monica was gone, she was much closer to official guardianship of Gabi than she would have imagined, and this strong, wonderful man was holding her as if he never wanted to let her go.

Happy didn't begin to cover it.

The old clock on the mantel chimed softly, a gentle sound in the quiet hush of the house. Oddly, she imagined she felt her grandfather's presence and she wished again that she'd had the chance to know him. A long, twisting road had led her to this moment, she thought, but right now she wouldn't have changed any step on that journey.

The chimes stopped and she looked out the window at the snowflakes drifting down through a moonbeam that must be shining through the clouds.

"It's midnight," she whispered. "Merry Christmas."

He kissed her again, his body warm and solid against hers. Perfect.

"I should go," he said after more long, delicious moments. "You need some sleep."

"Don't go."

He raised an eyebrow and she could feel herself blush. "That's not what I meant. Well, it's what I want, just not quite yet. I mean…"

He laughed and kissed her forehead. "I know what you mean."

"I still have to play Santa Claus and set out the presents I bought for Gabi. I want everything to be perfect. Her first real Christmas. I know how you feel about Christmas and I don't blame you a bit, but…would you stay and help me?"

"I can't think of anything else I'd like to do more."

He gave a slightly wicked smile. "Well, okay, I can think of a *few* things. But this will do for now."

He helped her carry the presents up from the corner of the dirt-floor cellar where she'd hidden them inside boxes. It took more trips than she had expected and she was surprised by the pile of presents that had collected over the past few weeks.

As they laughed and joked, setting things around the tree, she fell further and further in love with him. Just when she thought she couldn't be filled with more happiness, somehow she managed to find a little extra room inside.

When they finished the last trip, she stood back and looked beneath the tree, full from floor to bottom branches with presents.

"I'm afraid I might have gotten a bit carried away," she admitted. "I wrapped things as I bought them and I didn't catch the full impact until now, when I see them all together like this. Do you think it's too much?"

"I think it's just right. Gabi will be thrilled."

Grunt waddled over in front of the presents and plopped his hindquarters down, gazing at them both with an expectant sort of look.

Becca laughed. "Now, if only he would stay right there for the next five hours or so until she wakes up."

"Probably not much chance of that," he said with a smile of his own. "You're really into this, aren't you?"

"I never have been before. Christmas has always been just another day to get through. This year is different."

She paused, and for some ridiculous reason, she felt tears swell in her throat. "It's wonderful. The most perfect Christmas ever."

"I completely agree," he murmured, and kissed her again while the tree lights twinkled around them and the snow drifted down lightly outside and the ugly little dog looked on with an approving sort of smile.

* * * * *

HEART & HOME

Heartwarming romances where love can
happen right when you least expect it.

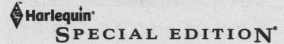

COMING NEXT MONTH
AVAILABLE NOVEMBER 22, 2011

#2155 TRUE BLUE
Diana Palmer

#2156 HER MONTANA CHRISTMAS GROOM
Montana Mavericks: The Texans Are Coming!
Teresa Southwick

#2157 ALMOST A CHRISTMAS BRIDE
Wives for Hire
Susan Crosby

#2158 A BABY UNDER THE TREE
Brighton Valley Babies
Judy Duarte

#2159 CHRISTMAS WITH THE MUSTANG MAN
Men of the West
Stella Bagwell

#2160 ROYAL HOLIDAY BRIDE
Reigning Men
Brenda Harlen

You can find more information on upcoming Harlequin® titles,
free excerpts and more at www.HarlequinInsideRomance.com.

HSECNM1111

*Lucy Flemming and Ross Mitchell shared a magical,
sexy Christmas weekend together six years ago.
This Christmas, history may repeat itself when they find
themselves stranded in a major snowstorm...
and alone at last.*

Read on for a sneak peek from
IT HAPPENED ONE CHRISTMAS
by Leslie Kelly.

Available December 2011, only from Harlequin® Blaze™.

EYEING THE GRAY, THICK SKY through the expansive wall of
windows, Lucy began to pack up her photography gear.
The Christmas party was winding down, only a dozen or so
people remaining on this floor, which had been transformed
from cubicles and meeting rooms to a holiday funland. She
smiled at those nearest to her, then, seeing the glances at her
silly elf hat, she reached up to tug it off her head.

Before she could do it, however, she heard a voice. A
deep, male voice—smooth and sexy, and so not Santa's.

"I appreciate you filling in on such short notice. I've
heard you do a terrific job."

Lucy didn't turn around, letting her brain process what
she was hearing. Her whole body had stiffened, the hairs on
the back of her neck standing up, her skin tightening into
tiny goose bumps. Because that voice sounded so familiar.
Impossibly familiar.

It can't be.

"It sounds like the kids had a great time."

Unable to stop herself, Lucy began to turn around,
wondering if her ears—and all her other senses—were
deceiving her. After all, six years was a long time, the mind

could play tricks. What were the odds that she'd bump into *him*, here? And today of all days. December 23.

Six years exactly. Was that really possible?

One look—and the accompanying frantic thudding of her heart—and she knew her ears and brain were working just fine. Because it was *him*.

"Oh, my God," he whispered, shocked, frozen, staring as thoroughly as she was. "Lucy?"

She nodded slowly, not taking her eyes off him, wondering why the years had made him even more attractive than ever. It didn't seem fair. Not when she'd spent the past six years thinking he must have started losing that thick, golden-brown hair, or added a spare tire to that trim, muscular form.

No.

The man was gorgeous. Truly, without-a-doubt, mouthwateringly handsome, every bit as hot as he'd been the first time she'd laid eyes on him. She'd been twenty-two, he one year older.

They'd shared an amazing holiday season.

And had never seen one another again.

Until now.

Find out what happens in
IT HAPPENED ONE CHRISTMAS
by Leslie Kelly.
Available December 2011, only from Harlequin® Blaze™